GIRTY

GIRTY

INTRODUCTION BY TED FRANKLIN BELUE

RICHARD TAYLOR

UNIVERSITY PRESS OF KENTUCKY

Editorial and Sales Offices: The University Press of Kentucky
663 South Limestone Street, Lexington, Kentucky 40508–4008
www.kentuckypress.com

ISBN 978-0-8131-8055-7 (hardcover : alk. paper)
ISBN 978-0-8131-8038-0 (paperback : alk. paper)
ISBN 978-0-8131-8039-7 (pdf)
ISBN 978-0-8131-8040-3 (epub)

Previously published in slightly different form in 1977, 1990, and 2006. The Library of
Congress has cataloged previous editions under Control Number 2005934272.

This book is printed on acid-free paper meeting
the requirements of the American National Standard
for Permanence in Paper for Printed Library Materials.

Manufactured in the United States of America.

Member of the Association of University Presses

In Memory of

Philip Richard Taylor
(1978-2003)

and

David Orr
(1942-1989)

And dedicated to

Philip Reuben Taylor,
my grandson

Preface

GIRTY **IS AN ATTEMPT** in fiction to reconstruct the life of Simon Girty (1741–1818), perhaps the most hated man in American history during much of the nineteenth century. Growing up on the frontier of western Pennsylvania, he was captured by the Indians and lived several years among the Senecas. At the time of the American Revolution, he was eking out a living as an interpreter at Fort Pitt, which we know now as Pittsburgh. For reasons not entirely clear, he sided with the British and Indians, beginning a lifelong career of resistance against the settlement of the Ohio River Valley and, more broadly, the old Northwest Territory. Historians with some justification have judged him a betrayer of his race, a renegade from the white civilization that was sweeping across the lands that touched "the Western Waters." Today others might regard him as an early defender of America's native cultures and the first white to take a strong stand on land use control in the Trans-Allegheny wilderness—a proto-conservationist.

The book is a collage of historical materials, including diaries, Indian captivities, travel accounts, guides, and biographies—a reconstruction of fragments, some heavily biased, that tell only part of the story. Girty himself tells the rest through a series of interior monologues divided between prose narratives and poems. The poems are intended to signal moments of transcendence or emotional intensity. Throughout there is an effort to depart from historical judgments and imagine Girty's life from his own perspective, working in the belief that history and fiction are distinguished mostly by differing degrees of subjectivity. Both disciplines reconstitute human experience, using levels of fact and illusion that are not always readily separated. The problem was compounded in Girty's case because he was illiterate. Not one word he actually uttered comes down to us reliably intact. What we know of him we must infer from reading his actions and the accounts written by a host of enemies and one or two friends.

Girty is not, I hope, simply an eastern western. Nor is there an attempt here to rehabilitate his character and the image his actions and history have created for him. My only intent is to let him speak for himself. A son of the border, he must permanently dwell in the borderland between legend and fact, one foot in each domain. The dated events, though they belong to history, are on loan. Girty's thoughts and perceptions, his emotions and allegiances, are emigrants from the frontier where fact slips easily back into myth and fiction.

Richard Taylor
October, 1989

Introduction

DANIEL BOONE was America's first frontier hero. In his day he received a lot of good press and became a living legend, the original Leatherstocking. To the mythmakers, Boone set the type: Nature's ultimate Natural Man, a noble white savage.

Simon Girty was America's first frontier villain. In his day he received a lot of bad press and became a living legend, the archetypal antihero and scurrilous renegade. To the myth-makers, Girty set the antitype: A truly savage White Savage.

Both men suffered captivity and loss at Indian hands. Deep in the heart of darkness, one man was nourished and turned philosophical; he became "an instrument ordained to settle the wilderness." The other succumbed to Eden's serpent and the Dark Side degraded him; turning traitor and race betrayer, he exchanged the white man's path for an inexorable slide into sadistic rapacity.

Neither image is true. Both images are true. "In a moral sense this man of the forest is purely a creation," said James Fenimore Cooper, sire of Leatherstocking.

Ironies abound. Boone and Girty befriended one another and in 1782 fought each other at Blue Licks and Girty's side bested Boone's, slaughtering one-thirteenth of Kentucky's militia in just under fifteen minutes. In 1778 both men swore loyalty oaths to become Britishers—albeit for a season in Boone's case. (In 1781 Boone again swore fealty to George III when Col. Banastre Tarleton's Rangers seized him in Charlottesville, Virginia). Both men adopted Indian skills and dress, ran with Indians, saw much to admire in Indian life.

Boone, reputed to be a great Indian slayer (an image he despised), said Indians treated him more fairly than whites, said he only killed three and those in self-defense. Girty, contrary to his malevolent celebrity, was blood-brother to famed woodsman Simon Kenton, saved a score of Americans from the stake, and purchased captive white boys from Indians to give to Brits to be educated and freed. In 1818 Girty died west of the Detroit River at British Fort Malden. In 1820 Boone died in Missouri. Both were buried with military honors.

It is a writer's task when dealing with such legends to winnow wheat from chaff to free the creature from the creation. Boone and Girty remain enigmas. Girty especially so. Boone books line shelves and steadily appear, but writers have given Girty short shrift; few have labored to understand him.

Even by frontier measure Girty came up hard. Born 1741 in the Pennsylvania border town of Chamber's Mill—"a settlement," biographer Consul Willshire Butterfield notes, "not famous for its morality"—he spent his youth woodsrunning, forting up to fusil fire, and eying Delaware and Shawnee hunters coming in summer with horses laden with deerskins, in winter with beaver and otter and mink pelts to barter with Girty, Sr., a trader and not a sober one. During a spree in a deal turned duel Samuel Saunders shot him. Another report says a Delaware named The Fish killed him. Girty, Jr., ten, saw it all.

In 1754 trader John Turner wed Mrs. Girty. Two years later French and Indian raiders torched Fort Granville and caught Turner. As Simon and his brothers—James, Thomas, George— watched, the warriors spent three hours burning their stepfather before skull-bashing him. To better make them into white Indians, the red men separated the Girty boys; for eight years Simon lived on Lake Erie's eastern shore in a Seneca long-house—a graduate course in survival and woodsmanship, ritual and diplomacy, politics and linguistics.

Freed after the French and Indian War, Girty was on his own hook, casting about from Fort Pitt and down the Ohio to the Illinois country, working as an interpreter for the British Indian Department and hiring out as a hunter to the Philadelphia firm Baynton, Wharton, and Morgan. He is "a Lad Who is particularly attach'd to me," wrote George Morgan, who extended him credit and sold him a rifle-gun. Tough, skilled, and fluent in eleven native tongues, Girty was a versatile man and one of Morgan's best-paid hands, but he quit after a raid in which, he reported, "thirty Indians had attackd our Boat & that no body had made their Escape"— except for himself.

A second lieutenant in the Virginia militia by 1775 (the end of Lord Dunmore's War) and go-between to the Grand Council of the Iroquois League on behalf of the new United States, it was during the Revolution that Girty the Patriot became Girty the White Savage. His will not easily bent to army discipline, deemed too friendly with Loyalists, defender of Indians and called a "drunk and unfit person," twice his superiors denied him a captain's commission. On March 28, 1778, Girty defected to the British Indian Department.

Frontier folk were shocked: Girty had "turned Indian" to loose the hell-hounds of war. In truth, Girty never commanded war parties but did serve as advisor and liaison to the British-allied Shawnee, Wyandot, and Mingo.

"He would raise hell to prevent peace," he told captive William May. True to his word, he did so. In 1779 Girty and some warriors besieged Ohio's Fort Laurens, killing twenty and thwarting a raid on Detroit, driving Americans back across the Ohio. In 1780 the partisans invaded Kentucky to seize Ruddle's and Martin's Stations. In 1781 Girty and a Wyandot band ravaged Squire Boone's Paint Lick Station; some reported sixty dead. In 1782 Simon watched Col. William Crawford burn at the stake; Dr. John Knight, a witness, said Girty mocked as Crawford danced on coals; other reports claim Girty presented Crawford with an escape plan which he rejected. Girty and company raided Bryan's Station that August, killing two and slaughtering livestock; two days later they ambushed 180 Americans at Blue Licks, killing seventy-seven. In 1791, for his valor in St. Clair's defeat, Simon was awarded the Americans cannons.

Infamy, deserved or not, was not long in coming—"the metaphysics of Indian hating," to quote Herman Melville.

"A no-good son of a bitch," Kentuckian Aaron Reynolds called Girty to his face but from behind fort walls. Moravian preacher John Heckewelder deemed him "as brutal, depraved, and wicked a wretch as ever lived." Ex-captive O. M. Spencer called him "the very picture of a villain." Frontier mothers scolded unruly children—"You be good or Dirty Dirty Simon Girty will get you." In 1791 Gen. Anthony Wayne offered $1000 for Girty's scalp.

By the time of his death in 1818, Girty's reputation had devolved into myth and legend. Like Boone, he became a malleable symbol, all things to all people. To Ohio Valley Indians, he was one of them. To the Brits he was a Loyalist. To Americans he was incarnate evil, a satanic emissary hell-bent upon white civilization's destruction. In 1840 Kentucky Governor James T. Morehead, in *An Address in Commemoration of the First Settlement of Kentucky*, spoke for his Manifest Destiny generation when he declared:

Girty became an Indian by adoption—acquired their habits—participated in their deliberations—inflamed their passions—and goaded them on to deeds of human atrocity. I called him an incendiary. He was worse—he was a monster. No famished tiger ever sought the blood of a victim with more unrelenting rapacity, than Girty sought the blood of the white man.

The *Missouri Gazette*, May 7, 1814, reported that Girty's character " 'of being a savage, unrelenting monster,' is much exaggerated." That he was an honest man who paid his debts, but "Indian in his manners." In 1890 Robert Clarke publishers released Consul Butterfield's *History of the Girtys*, which remains "definitive" though unbalanced, claims California writer Phillip Hoffman, who believes Butterfield exploited Girty's notoriety. "He's the most maligned Colonial I can think of. Nobody was more vilified than he was." Hoffman concludes, "when the facts are considered, Girty emerges deserving of much respect and admiration for his convictions, principles, and bravery."

Girty fares as well (or less so) in Theodore Roosevelt's Anglo-Saxon conquest apologia, *The Winning of the West* (1907), and so it goes in the twentieth century, Girty the villain of drama, books, and film. In 1936 celluloid Boone (cherubic, well-fed George O'Brien) squared off against celluloid Girty (swarthy, reed-thin John Carradine) in director David Howard's low-budget assault upon history, *Daniel Boone*. Howard, though, remains a pioneer of pioneer imagery: His Boone rescues distressed damsels and looks dashing in his 'coon-skin cap while nemesis Girty skulks, scowls, menaces women, and wears a cap of skunk skin.

Today Girty is mostly forgotten, but his name lives on in rather curious ways. "Girty's Notch" is a locally famous rock cropping on the western bank of the Susquehanna, south of Liverpool, Pennsylvania; Girty, rumor has it, slept in a cave there but no one is sure which one. In Upper Sandusky, there are two monuments in memory of Col. William Crawford, for whom Crawford County, Ohio, was named; a sign indicates where he died. "Simon Girty" appears on a road marker near Lexington, Kentucky, commemorating the siege of Bryan's Station. In June 2001 Pennsylvanians erected a Girty historical marker near Harrodsburg; on hand for its unveiling was Ken Girty, Simon's great-great-great-great-great nephew who told reporters, "I think he was great. Just misunderstood." Academics Colin G. Calloway (*Simon Girty: Interpreter and Intermediary*, 1989) and Richard Slotkin (*Regeneration through Violence: The Mythology of the American Frontier, 1600–1800*, 1973) have done much to burnish Girty's image. An effort long due.

So it is that I am pleased to see this edition of Richard Taylor's *Girty*, a profound little book I discovered in 1989 or so. When I want to read writing truly done, I read *Girty*, a poetic foray into a Dark and Bloody Ground that couples man and myth, romantic hero and implacable antihero. Iconoclastic in its tack, elegiac and spare in its lyricism, no other work on this singular man who was both so loved and reviled hits the mark so well and gives him a reason for being.

Ted Franklin Belue
September 11, 2005
Murray, Kentucky

GIRTY

"The jury Mr. Webster demands," said the stranger, sipping at his boiling glass. "You must pardon the rough appearance of one or two, they will have come a long way."

And with that the door blew open and twelve men entered one by one.

If Jabez Stone had been sick with terror before, he was blind with terror now. For there was Walter Butler, the Loyalist, who spread fire and horror through the Mohawk Valley in the times of the Revolution; and there was Simon Girty, the renegade, who saw white men burned at the stake and whooped with the Indians to see them burn. His eyes were green like a catamount's, and the stains on his hunting shirt did not come from the blood of deer.

The Devil and Daniel Webster
Stephen Vincent Benet

In the Findlay (0.) Courier, published some years since, it is asserted that, "A short time ago, a dirk-knife was found embedded in the center of a tree on the farm of Alexander Morrison, about 3 miles northeast of Findlay. On being cleaned there was found on the blade of the knife, rudely cut, the letters 'S. Girty, 1782.' "This, however, I have not been able to verify.

History of the Girtys
Consul Willshire Butterfteld

It has frequently been said that it is impossible to make a white man out of an Indian, but very easy to make an Indian of a white man, the history of the Girtys illustrates the latter.

Trans-Allegheny Pioneers
John H. Hale

Late Summer, 1756

MY INITIATION to the Delawares comes through a hole burned in the stockade at Fort Granville. This sad excuse for a fortification stands, or stood, between the Juniata River and Sherman Creek on the Susquehanna. A ramshackle square of cabins joined by logs laid horizontally, maybe 8 feet high. This flimsy wall and 20 militiamen are the only protection between us and about 100 Delawares and Shawnees led by some French. Us being my mother, my stepfather John Turner, my three natural brothers and one step, and some dozen or so neighbors, mostly Lacefields and Bartletts.

Burning the hole is easy, done almost before we see the smoke. The lay of the fort is such that a deep ravine runs from the river up to a few feet of the pickets. This ravine, overgrown with brush and saplings, gives them cover enough to fire it fast and secret, blue flames gnawing a 6-foot gap before we can dump our first bucket. The fighting quickly centers on this spot. From behind the window where I am crouching I see several Canadians and Indians shot as they rush through, cut down in our crossfire. But some of ours fall too, including Armstrong, who was left in charge when that simpleton Captain Ward took most of the men to guard the wheat reapers in Sherman Valley. Which is why, of course, they pick now to attack. As the fighting grows hotter, one by one those holding the gap are killed, beets sprouting out of their foreheads, chests filled with thimble-sized holes.

Then out of this confusion—the smoke, the gunfire, the women bellowing—steps the chief frog. Half-hidden behind a tree, a squat dandy wearing spotless white breeches shouts in fragile English for us to give up. There really isn't much choice since most of the men are either dead or dying. The Frenchman offers quarter and solemnly promises to hold off his Indians. This decision is left up to my stepfather John Turner, who inherited the command from Armstrong ten minutes before. One look around the fort, the litter of dead and bleeding, and he just throws down the gate, leaving us to their mercy. Which is not much. The instant our weapons are down, a dozen assassins dash in and tomahawk the wounded, including our nearest neighbor, an old man named Brandon. No one lifts a hand to stop the slaughter. The Frenchman is nowhere in sight. After this first furious cruelty, they become more select, singling out those too old or feeble for work, killing and scalping them also. The rest, those of us still with breath in our bodies, are turned into pack mules and loaded with nearly our own weight in plunder. I am forced to tote an enormous brass kettle. John Turner I remember staggering under a hundred-pound sack of salt. In one afternoon my whole family falls captive—John Turner, my mother, Baby John, my brothers Tom and George and James.

Three days later we reach Kittanning, a large Delaware town up the Allegheny. The whole village turns out for the homecoming, cheering their husbands, their fathers, their brothers, taunting and stoning the prisoners. Never have I seen so many people in one place. Hordes of gawking onlookers dressed in knee-length leather frocks or near naked, menacing crow-black eyes set in skin the color of tobacco. There are 50 or so lodges, rude cabins mostly, and some tents made of hides. We are led to a clearing in the center of the village. Here we are tied to posts to be offered as sport to the squaws and urchins who stayed behind. Swinging willow whips and clubs, they beat us for a solid hour during a general holiday.

At Kittanning my mother is made a widow for the second time. Widowed from the man who murdered the Delaware named The Fish, who made her a widow the first time. The triangle stretches into a square. It so happens the chief of this town is a one-eyed terror named Tewea, pronounced "Too-way," This Tewea, better known as Captain Jacobs, is The Fish's brother, and the last time he saw his brother alive he was setting out with a boodle of skins to trade with my father and John Turner, who were, in more ways than one it was said, partners. The question is whether Tewea remembers. He acknowledges that he does by smashing John Turner in the mouth and ordering a large fire.

So at Kittanning up the Allegheny my brothers and me are orphaned for a second time as our stepfather roasts before our eyes. We all expect the same treatment, but fortunately Tewea considers the score evened. And besides, he has other plans for us. No fool, he knows we are worth more to him alive than dead. So after much squabbling among the tribesmen, we are parcelled out to separate villages for adoption, the idea being for us to replace those killed during the attack on Granville. We are split up because we will lose our white ways sooner, none of us being considered blood-poisoned enough (I, next to eldest, am 15) to be beyond correction.

Tom and George are sent to Goschachgunk, a Delaware village at the fork of the Muskingum River. James, my mother and her baby, to a Shawnee town on the Scioto (Elk River) in the Ohio country. Me, to Cattaraugus in New York where the Senecas adopt me not long before I adopt them. Safe back on their homeground and fat with plunder, they leave me pretty much on my own. Once I know they mean to adopt me, I put aside Chambers' Mill and begin a life not so different from what I'm accustomed to. Indian ways come easy. The life is no harder, no crueler than life with my father. The food, better and more abundant. The free life suits me.

That spring, before the oak leaves are the size of a squirrel's ear, I am adopted into the tribe. This is a solemn event and the whole village turns out for the ceremony. How it is done. First, some old women strip and beat me with willow switches just short of drawing blood. This to stir up the impure spirits in my body. Next they drag me to water where the white blood is scrubbed from my skin with sharp gravel and sand from the sacred bottom of the Allegheny River. Along the banks the whole tribe stands witness. The sachems look on from high ground, old men sucking their hollow clay pipes, some muttering and thumping a deerskin drum. When their chanting dies off, one old waster, toothless and drawn up in the face, pulls my ear to his face and whispers my secret name. He tells me I have become one of "The People."

So starts my first three years with the Senecas, the Maechachtinni, grandchildren of the Sun and the Moon. The white blood washes off easier than dirt. Most of the time I am free to hunt. When I am not hunting, I am eating or sleeping. The language comes slower. The words, which sound at first like the grunts of rutting brutes, break up at last into separate sounds and meanings. Though I pick up words soon enough, they are not understood when I try to speak until I learn to draw them from deep in my chest and pass them through my nose. The secret is in the breath. Soon I have the sounds for most things and know to point to others. From the time I can speak, my acceptance is complete. The rest comes easy. Wearing a loincloth, acquiring a taste for stewed dog and boiled mussels, an eagle feather tied to my scalplock, my white skin greased and gaudy, my career beginning. Rub a sheep against pitch, he gits up with tar.

John Turner

They paint his body black.
They tie him to a post.
They strike some flint to start a fire
and dance around his feet.
They heat their barrels
in the flames
and push them in his flesh.
They draw their knives
and lift his scalp
then wave it in my face.
My second father's death-song
is longer than my first's.
He gripes, he whines
he runs the scale.
He whimpers on each fret
of pain
till Tewea lifts his six-year-old
who plants a hatchet in his brain.

Vita

Name: Simon Girty, Jr. Sometimes spelled Girtee, Gerty, or Girte. Also known among the Delaware as Katepacomen from a ceremony in which a chief by that name exchanged names with him to do him honor. Whites know him as "The White Indian" and "The Great Renegade."

Birthplace: Chambers' Mill at Paxtang (Paxton) on Fishing Creek on the east side of the Susquehanna five miles above Harrison's (now Harrisburg), Lancaster County, Colony of Pennsylvania. Born 1741; under what sign, no one knows. Died 18th of February, 1818, at his farm near Fort Malden, two miles out of Amherstburg, County of Essex, Province of Upper Canada. Aged 77. Buried with military honors as a loyal subject of Great Britain. As he died in the winter, his remains had to be lifted over his fence, the gate being blocked by snow-banks. A farm-gate is said to swing over his grave.

Father: Simon Girty, Sr. Deceased. An Irish immigrant. Occupation: pack-horse driver, Indian trader, general sot. "Nothing ranked higher in his estimation, or so entirely commanded his regard, as a jug of whisky." Cause of death: a tomahawk blow to the head administered by a Delaware named No-me-tha, "The Fish," during a spree.

Mother: Mary Newton Girty. An Englishwoman, twice widowed. Birth and death dates unknown. Children: Thomas (b. 1739);

Simon; James (b. 1743); and George (b. 1745). Remarried to John Turner, her deceased husband's partner, who was burned at the stake in 1755. One child of that union: John Turner, Jr. (b. 1754). Mary died obscurely in the vicinity of Pittsburgh.

Permanent Address: Northwest Territory, Ohio River Valley, c.o. General Henry Hamilton, "The Hair-buyer," Lieutenant-Governor of Canada, Fort Detroit. After 1795, at his home near Malden. For a few years during the '90s, at Girty's Town, his trading camp in northwestern Ohio.

Description: Stands about 5'9." A heavy frame, short neck. Full, round face. Raven-black hair, shaggy. Dark, dark eyes. The lip, thin and compressed. Distinguishing marks: a diagonal scar made by a saber slash across the forehead. Most typically dressed in Indian costume but without any ornament, a silk handkerchief taking the place of a hat, wound about the head pirate-style to hide the wound. A knee-length buckskin frock with fringes. One silver mounted pistol stuck in his elkskin belt on each side. These said to have belonged to Colonel David Rogers of Virginia. Hanging on the left side, a short, broad dirk which serves occasionally the uses of a knife. "His intemperance, and the scar upon his forehead, marred, to some extent, his features. It cannot be said, however, that he was a repulsive-looking man. In his prime, he was very agile." Only one likeness has come down.

Religion: If any, a simple trust in the provision of The Great Spirit.

Education: Three years among the Senecas at Cattaraugus in New York. General woodcraft, hunting and trapping, elementary rifle repair. A good sense of territory and direction. A star reader. Also a student of signs. Foreign languages: Seneca, Wyandot, Delaware. Enough Shawanese to be understood.

Occupation: Indian interpreter, ex-Lieutenant in the Continental Army, scout, counselor and confidant of the Wyandot Indians, Iroquois confederacy. Agent and interpreter for the Crown. Scrupulously honest as a trader, having utterly no interest in the acquisition of property, having never made a claim until he was over forty, married, and seeking refuge and a home in Canada. This at a time when land fever was the prevalent disease of the West.

Wife: Catherine Malott. Sometimes spelled Malotte. White, born somewhere in Maryland. Described at one time as the most beautiful woman in Detroit. Captured by an offshoot clan of Delaware Indians at 15, with whom she lived as an adopted member until meeting and marrying Girty in 1784, Girty being over twice her age, forty-two. Children: Ann (b. 1786), Thomas (b. 1788); Sarah (b. 1791); and Prideaux (b. 1797). Died 1852. The three children who survived her lived "thoroughly respectable" lives.

An Estimate of What Girty's Life Has to Teach Young Readers

'**IT** WOULD BE WELL IF THE NAME OF THIS MONSTER could be erased from the annals of Kentucky, unless it may be assumed that some good can accrue to the young from a knowledge of how fiendish even a white man may become when he puts himself outside of the pale of Christian civilization. His life presents nothing to be imitated; and it can hardly be said that a picture so demoniac is necessary in this enlightened age to awaken those feelings of strong reprobation which incline the inexperienced to shun the paths that lead to cruelty and crime. ... The young reader who prosecutes the study of the history of Kentucky will find that his associates from boyhood were brutal savages, and that he was more brutal than they; that his hatred of the pioneers was more satanic than that of the red men who believed that the white man was their natural enemy. ... It would be unprofitable to give the details of his murderous career. He died in Canada, opposite Detroit, in old age, poor, despised, and miserable; or, as others assert, in battle at the Thames."

Thompson's *Young People's History of Kentucky*, 1897

Girty Contemplates the World of Letters

I stare at the page,
the words like tiny boots
their heels in snow,
tracks I can't make or follow.
Words fur my head.
They weave thick weaves
and pelt my bones.
They shrivel when I stretch.
My comfort to know
you will know me not by tracks
but only by some skins
I've shed.

BUTLER

Fort Pitt

THE THREE OF THEM getting the best of Girty now. All of them panting, the three in uniform and the one on the ground, a swart gypsy-looking man bleeding about the mouth, one eye swollen shut, the good eye the furious eye of a madman. An interpreter at the fort. When he falls, the officer, a beefy lieutenant named Williamson, moves in border-style and lifts his boot to stomp some ribs.

This is when the stranger Butler horns in. And not some pipsqueak either, but a hulking figure of a man. And young, maybe 19. The complexion of matters changing as he brings the rifle to bear on the officer's chest. Who, not sure what to do, does nothing. Just goes stockstill. All of them imitating him when the hammer clicks, cocked and ready. Sun just singing off that blue oiled barrel, busy off the brassy scrolls along the stock.

Then, without one syllable uttered, it's over. The three backing off, slinking back in the crowd like water into sand, eyes still locked on the muzzle, focused on the pea-sized hole inside the octagon, as the underdog, the one Williamson called Indian-lover, wipes the gore from his mouth to say how-do, the stranger owning his name is Butler as the gypsy smiles his gypsy smile. A crow's jump from death.

The Meadow

SHOT THIS MORNING A FINE RED BUCK. Twelve points. Having slept in some beeches, I wake to sounds of a squirrel cutting, his long incisors gnawing small bitter beechnuts somewhere close. Breakfast. Cocking and priming, quiet as I can I settle back in my robes to spy him out, my sight fixed on leaf-ends as the uppermost glow out of the half-light and burn white along the edges, trunks still steaming. And wait. A quarter hour later brother squirrel and I both sense some third presence, the feel of some interloper moving over my body like waves. Then the hush. For a moment or two everything goes stony as we listen: insects, squirrel, twitter of thrushes, even yesterday's shower mammering in the branch. Then as evenly starts up again.

Some minutes pass before I see him. Thirty paces off, head bent in the browse, a fat buck grazing his way through the high grass which abounds in the clearing. This clearing, a meadow not much larger than the shade of a sizeable tree, is to my right, now fortunately upwind. Peculiar the way he moves and chews, methodically and cautious, raising his head now and then to catch my scent, but doesn't. He is so close I can see the dark wet dew line on his forelegs, parts of him still vague in the blue film sunlight is cutting now. The antler tree sprouting out of his crown rolls in time with the working of his jaws. Fickle, he tries one delicacy, then another, gathering salads, his arched neck deftly yanking and twisting the forage from its roots. His winter coat he has not shed yet. It's matted and shaggy, the color of dry bark, parts of it stuccoed with flaky mud. I can just make out the ring of dung beneath his tail.

Careful not to spook him, I maneuver my body into a line with his, bringing my weapon to bear. I draw a gradual bead to the center of his chest just above the jointure of the forelegs, then slowly squeeze. But my aim is off. The ball strikes slightly higher, entering right of center, and penetrates the upper neck. Ordinarily this would not stop him dead though he would likely bleed to death in some thicket several miles away. Yet this time it is enough. Too late, he pitches and bounds toward the brush. The ball must have sliced his vitals, for he wavers even while his reflexes gather the muscles into flight, gaining speed only to crumple twenty or so paces away in deep clover. Mortal.

I move toward him as if under water, my ears still swarming with the shot, that high-pitched paining sound that fills my head like a hemorrhage. When I reach him, the tremors are already in his extremities, legs stiffening in awkward jerks, large buck eyes glazing. The hooves, fine and sharp as chisels, even sharper now, have that clumsy look things take on as they are separated from their functions, lose their grace. Bending closer, I find the knot of blue-stem stuck between the front teeth, still dewed. Life and death flop in my head. Life and death. I see the long jaws chewing and now still, the yellowed glint of the cuspids with their chaw of green. My hand, no longer mine, moving by some instinct of its own to my side where the knife is. The same hand pressing the blade to cut out the tongue and liver, delicacies. Both being warm yet, more live than dead, they steam. These and some fillets from the tender part of the shoulder are all I can carry. The rest I must leave for the buzzards. Times I have seen the creeks fill with carcasses, bloated does minus one steak or a tongue. Next,

I strike a fire, skewering some choice on a green stick, roasting it brown and dripping. This, with the last of my parched corn, makes a passable breakfast.

Full, I stuff what's left in my pouch, remembering to cut enough sinew from the shank to re-string my moccasins. The grass nearly dry as I gather my gear to move on. The carcass already drawing its wreath of flies. Crickets fretting their thighs inside my head. Sun inching higher. Not a gesture of cloud in the sky. Neither hearing or seeing the squirrel.

The Cave

I CAN STILL SEE THE CAVE. Really more a pocket than a cave, a rock shelter not even high enough to stand, sides slabbed with smooth blue rock and parched as only rainless places are. You will find it up the Muskingum where Kenton and I spied for Lord Dunmore during his campaign to destroy the Wapatomica towns. Which you will not find. These months spent running messages, reading signs, scouting the flanks on marches, and the like.

The two of us put up here for the night. Snug in comfort's lap. In the puny light late this afternoon Kenton bagged two gobblers, and the soft parts of one are roosting in my belly. The bones I am sucking for their marrow, which the Wyandots call "war food." There is a pile of them between us, snapped, white, and stringy. Firelight is lipping off the rocks, air just cold enough to see our breath if we crawl outside. We are relaxed now, moccasins stretched toward the fire, splinters of damp making little spits in the flames.

Two weeks in the wilds together, sharing kills, eyes skinned for sign, our senses whittled and honed to work as single instinct. Simon and Simon. Both of us Simons. It was Butler then, not Kenton, though I didn't know this yet. The Indians say it "Bahd-lar." Calls himself Butler because he murdered, or so he believed, a man back in Fauquier County, Virginia, where his daddy worked a piddling farm. Over a girl, he told me later. Sixteen and lovestruck, big even then, he jumped his rival, beat him until he fell, and left him for dead in a cornfield, heading for the outlands to escape the law. Years before he learned the man was alive and married to the sweetheart.

It is getting colder now and tending the fire occupies us both. Bold yellow light fills the shelter, throwing shifty patterns on the roof and walls where bits of mineral in the rock catch the glint and hold it in sparkling crystals. I feel the palm of heat even on my face and hands, warmth sifting through my gut and limbs. The coals as they breathe and deepen forming little gray crusts as what consumes them moves inward feeding on itself, white ashes banking in fragile piles, each log withering into charcoal in the hot white flames. Our eyes fastened on this lung of coals. Out of time. Or maybe inside its rhythms, as the jumpy light bends off rocks and works its spell on us, leaving reservoirs of black shadow in the pits and crevices. Content, at one, these are not the words. Neither speaking nor needing to, the fire drawing us in from its fringes, binding us stronger than any rope. Bound as we are in rags of smoke, the musky smell of burning wood and turkey grease, heat welling through our insides like wind through nets. Never, before or since, have I confessed feeling so close to another of my own kind.

Then I remember how the Senecas join themselves by mingling bloods and ask why we don't do the same. Sure, he says, but he's not certain how. I tell him with blood, drawing my knife from the sheath at my side. I explain to him how our bloods must join and flow as one stream, how the joining will make us brothers. In the guttering light, he rolls his sleeve to expose the wrist and its map of green veins which branch and fork like tributaries of a river. The skin on the underside of his forearm incredibly white, womanly.

So now I apply the blade-tip to the flat of his forearm, only denting it at first, then increasing the pressure till the red shows.

Now doing the same to mine. Feeling the pressure against my wrist, the tiny burr as it furrows the skin, creased crimson trailing. Only afterward do the nerves dispatch their small messages of pain, the cells raising their voices in alarm through my body. Next, pressing my pulse to his so the bloods blend. Reading his eyes, building the image in my consciousness part by part, holding all of it for one long solemn minute.

When it is over, I explain how we have pledged ourselves to protect the other, no matter the odds, so long as either breathes. How we are brothers now, Simon and Simon. Each of us swears, and I know he means it. This done, I bring the flask from my wallet to seal the pledge. When I offer him a drink, he refuses, saying he don't know how he'll go, but it won't be from barrel fever. And both of us laughing, the liquor scorching as I swallow, its rivulets of fire irrigating me. Already I feel its oven-warmth spread slowly through my limbs, soothing the smart in my wrist, dousing for a time this spark that glows in my throat, the ember which never dies. I am on my way to the altitudes. I study my breath as, drawn to the cooler air, it melts in the lift of woodsmoke outside.

The Squaw Campaign:
February, 1778

AN EEL ON A LOG IN THE RIVER. Midwinter. The log is maybe 50 yards out, its slippery black trunk and branch stubs pencilled against the dull expanse of water which sucks and tugs the soupy light above the shoreline. The river is glazed a drab gray as if smeared on the landscape with a knife. Its surface is broken only by occasional chunks of uprooted trees and scribbling eddies that twirl and vanish between the swells. The eel itself is coiled around some root-ends as if to fix its grip against the current which jounces the log and bobs it like a cork.

Someone farther down the line sees it first and starts the firing. A minute later 20 or so rifles take up the challenge and soon the whole army, 500 strong, is taking potshots at the lump of twined muscle, which the distance makes no larger than the thongs on their mocassins, determined to kill it before it can drift out of sight. Even the officers, at first standing idle, join the competition, cradling their muskets in the crotches of trees to steady their aim.

Though the expedition has not been a success, neither has it been a failure. The men are in high spirits, glad to be heading home. What began as a major campaign into the Indian country takes on the character of a junket in the woods. This is how it happens. Brigadier-General Edward Hand, the commander at Ft. Pitt, hears that some boatloads of supplies were cached by the British at an Indian camp on the Cuyahoga River. He gathers a force of volunteers and sets out to capture them. Girty signs on as scout. Though the march proceeds well for the first several days, the weather takes a turn as heavy rains and snowmelt oblige them to stop 20 miles above the mouth of the Beaver on the Mahoning. Miles short of their destination. Here Girty discovers some Indian tracks, their number and course indicating a war party intent on raiding the settlements. The trail leads back to a camp estimated to contain 50 to 60 Indians.

Forming his men in a skirmish line, General Hand attacks the village only to find it abandoned, or mostly so. After a one-sided fight, he manages to capture one man and a handful of stragglers, women and children. The Indian and one of the squaws are clubbed to death before he can restrain his men. He saves the life of another by personally taking her into his custody. The others escape.

Questioned through Girty who knows the language, the surviving prisoner, a grandmother so palsied she could not keep up with the others, informs them that they have taken a camp of the Munceys, a clan of the Delawares. The menfolk, she tells them, are making salt 10 miles farther up the Mahoning. Hand elects to stay in camp but immediately dispatches a force to take the remaining Munceys, reported to number 10 braves. Girty, familiar with the country since his days with the Senecas, leads them to the salt lick. Reaching the site, the party surrounds and captures all the enemy, the warriors transforming into four women and a boy, "of whom," Hand reports, "one woman only was saved." In the process, one man, a captain, is wounded—whether by one of the women or the boy is not stated. Another man is drowned.

For a time it appears that the eel, sticking steadfast to his stump, will float out of range of the volunteers' rifles. As the firing mounts from random shots to a single, incessant fusillade, scarves of blue smoke swaddle the sycamores and brush-piles along the bank. Though the log is gradually reduced to splintery pulp, almost miraculously the eel is not hit. The firing continues until the sodden heartwood has enough lead in it to sink, but for some reason doesn't. Shots wide of the mark kick up little geysers, which rise and fall harmlessly around it like pebbles thrown by a child. Finally, just when it seems the eel will escape unharmed, a last volley strikes home, the eel disintegrating before their eyes like wood chips from the cleft of an ax. Hooraws.

Safely returned to Ft. Pitt, General Hand describes this first expedition into the Indian country during the Revolution as a "great exploit."

For the first and only time in his career, Girty marches under the flag of his countrymen against the Indians.

March 27, 1778

THE NIGHT OF MARCH 27TH, 1778, I TAKE A STAND. Which is to go. Going is neither hard nor hazardous. At midnight I simply unbar the gates and slip out for our rendezvous at McKee's Rocks, the farm belonging to Alexander McKee, ex-Indian agent at the fort and trusted servant of the King. There, besides McKee, I find Matt Elliott, Robert Surphlit (who is McKee's cousin), a blacksmith named Higgins nobody knows too well, and McKee's two Negroes. Seven of us in all. All heading for Detroit to side with the British and Indians. McKee has been planning elopement for years and knows the route through Indian country almost as well as I do.

From McKee's Rocks we ride west through the Ohio territory, having several run-ins with the Indians but without any mishaps. When some Shawnees overtake us near Pluggy's Town, they know us for friends, as I am an adopted Seneca, a cousin. We get to Detroit in early June and give what Hamilton calls "satisfactory assurances of our fidelity to his Majesty's cause." This is not hard since our names are already on his secret list of loyal subjects. He merely checks our identities. Turns out he has uses for all of us. McKee and Elliott are given commissions straightaway. Because I know Indians and speak several dialects, I am hired as an interpreter. My salary is 16 shillings, York currency, and 1 and ½ rations per day. I am also given a flintlock rifle, a saddle and bridle, and three horses. Then I am assigned to the Mingoes. These Mingoes are a bastard tribe made up of misfits, half-breeds, and renegades, cast-offs from all the tribes. Bachelors' sons, every one. They make me welcome. From this time on, I quit being an American.

No one quite knows how to explain why a white man could choose to live among heathens, among Indians, and adopt their ways so completely as to turn on his own race. This bothers them since it suggests something is wrong with *them*. They drum their minds for reasons and this is what they come up with:

1) Not being paid by the Virginia House of Burgesses for my scout to learn the temper or the Wyandots;
2) Bearing a grudge against Col. George Morgan who hired me as fort interpreter at a salary of 5/8's of a dollar per day "during good behavior or the pleasure of the Hon. Continental Congress" and fired me 3 months later for undefined "ill-behavior."
3) Plunder-love;
4) Being trounced by Gen. Andrew Lewis with a cane, the traditional account stating that the day before his own trouncing at Point Pleasant I came to him expecting payment for my scouting. When he refused, hot words were exchanged and he struck me about the head with his cane. I am reported to have said, "D—n you, sir, your quarters shall swim in blood for this," before deserting to Cornstalk and guiding his attack the next day.
5) Being soft on redskins, especially the women;
6) Being seduced by British gold;
7) Simply following the tendencies of my nature, which are variously described as bloodthirsty, unpitying, cruel, fiend-like, brutal, depraved, and wicked. I am known as a dark whirlwind of fury, desperation, and barbarity, an untaught creature with

the face of a white man and the heart of an Indian; a relentless barbarian; an inveterate drunkard; a desperado, the base deserter of my native land; a blustering ruffian; an untutored savage, a turncoat, a wretched miscreant; an incendiary; a monster of cruelty; a host of evil spirits; a prince of treachery; an anomaly of western history; a savage in everything but color; the terror of women, the bugaboo of children.

All of the above are true. None of the above are true. Who wants to know? What difference does it make? I did it. Human motives, mine at least, reduce to several laws. I am my only fort. Plug your wounds with buzzard down. Test your powder when it rains. Cats draw lightning. Crows make poor umbrellas.

Meeting Kenton, Chillicothe

I DON'T KNOW HIM AT FIRST HE LOOKS SO SORRY. His body is one large unbandaged wound, bruised and swollen, hammered out of shape like beaten tin. His face and chest, his arms and legs are painted black, smudged with charcoal and bear grease. His whole body is caked with soot, even down to the hair which I would recognize as his. He is cut-ta-ho-tha. Condemned.

When I enter the council house, a long low log building in the center of the village, he is slumped against the wall with the others waiting judgment. I ask him, as I asked the others, if he is from south of the Ohio. He nods yes. I ask him how many men there are in Kentucky. He tells me it's impossible to reckon but that he can name the officers and their respective ranks so I can judge for myself. He names me names, though I recognize this for a ruse since every simpleton knows the militia in Kentucky is top-heavy with officers, the colonels all but outnumbering the privates. I tell him as much. To test his information, I ask him if he knows William Stewart. Which he does, well. So I ask his name, and he raises his head slowly, lips cracking a smile through the black crust around his mouth. Whoever thought, he says, the day would come when my own brother don't know me. I can only stare harder into the grayish eyes, the pupils smaller in the half-light of the lodge, windowless but for a smoke-hole in the roof. Butler, he says, Simon Butler.

Butler! The name sinks into my skull like a hatchet, strikes me dumb. It dawns on me now. Butler! I know him. My arms about his head, the tears already welling in my eyes. Simon Butler.

I listen while he tells his story. How he and two others, desiring some sport, decided to make their own maraud across the Ohio to steal Shawnee horses. Traveling as far as they dared during the day, on the third afternoon they put up near Chillicothe where they located a large pasture in which the horses were kept. They laid low in a canebrake a mile or so away and waited for nightfall. Just at sundown, when the shadows were long but not so dark they could miss their way, each in turn crawled to the corral and roped three horses, using salt to lure them to the edge of the meadow where the others were concealed. Everything went as planned. So far, so good.

When each had his horses, they strung them three to a man and hightailed back to the Ohio. They took the usual precautions to cover their tracks by traveling streambeds and sticking to hard ground, knowing there would be pursuers. When they reached the river, their luck ran out, for the wind riffled the water too high and the horses wouldn't cross white water. They waited till evening hoping for a change, but the wind did not let up. Itchy now, they devised another plan, which was to follow the shoreline downriver until they reached the Falls where the water was fordable. Instead, the trackers overtook them, scalping Montgomery and capturing him. The third man, a tenderfoot named Clarke, escaped by swimming the river.

Furious, Butler's five captors, one of them the notorious Red Pole, beat him hollow, taunting him as "hoss-steal." When they are finished, both eyes are pinched closed by puffy skin, both badly blacked. A nasty cut runs down one cheek from ear to chin. For more amusement, they straddle him backwards on the meanest horse, tie his arms around the neck and his ankles around the belly. Then, with switches they prod the horse through nettles and scrub. After a mile he is bleeding from wounds all over his body. Three days it takes them to reach Chillicothe. Each step of the way, branches and brush cut him terribly, almost blind him. Each night they stake him out spread-eagle, arms, legs, and neck bound to rawhide straps fastened to pegs, the pegs driven deep.

When they arrive at Chillicothe, one of the principal Shawnee towns, he is forced to run the gauntlet twice. The crowd of women and children, everyone in the village, parts to form a corridor down which he must run while being struck with clubs and bare fists. At the end of the course is a post which he must clasp before the beating is stopped. The second time he runs he is knocked unconscious halfway to the post. When he comes to, he is tried as a horse thief under Shawnee law, found guilty, and sentenced to burn at the stake, the execution to be postponed so he can be paraded in other towns and run still other gauntlets.

To Piqua town on Mad River he went. Then farther north to Wapatomica and Mackachack's town. He became a whipping boy, a target for every man's grief or hatred. At each village he ran the gauntlet. At each he was struck with everything from willow wands to flattened hatchets. Helpless, he was spit on and urinated on. At Moluntha's town he nearly escaped, breaking the aisle of squaws and children, outrunning the entire tribe only to run smack into a hunting party on horseback led by Chief Blue Jacket, himself a white, who rode him down and dented his skull with a hatchet. He woke two days later back in Moluntha's town where he was given some rest in preparation for his final ordeal.

After a few days a second council was held and again he was pronounced cut-ta-ho-tha. Again he ran the gauntlet and again he was knocked unconscious, this time by a club which glanced off his earlier skull-wound. He woke staked out on the ground. He bit meat from the rump of a fat squaw who tried to defecate on his head. He watched elaborate preparations for his own barbecue as old women set a locust post in the ground and stacked faggots around it several feet high. By this time he wanted to die. Anything to release him from the pain and abuse. He was surprised he had lasted this long. He knew his luck couldn't hold and that he was in no condition to help himself. In the end he resigned himself and spent most of his time memorizing the mesh of leaves and limbs against the sky.

This is his situation when I return from the Kentucky raid and find him in the lodge. Then we are no longer there. We are back that winter on the Muskingum, back in the cave by the fire. The knife is between us and I am staring at the crimson thread on my wrist as it widens and runs. I know that I must make a speech.

Turning toward the judges, I palm my heart to show from where the words come. First, so there will be no misunderstandings, I remind them that I am one of them, having proved my loyalty a thousand times. That I cannot be suspected of favoring the whites since I have just brought 7 white scalps from Kentucky. That I have sworn to fight until the last white man is expelled from The Middle Ground. Next, and this with emotion, that I have given my oath that Butler is my brother and must not be killed, that to kill him is to kill me. I tell them how he saved my life at Ft. Pitt when the soldiers attacked me and how we pledged ourselves on the Muskingum. How he would give his life to save mine and how I will give my life to save his should that price be demanded. Finally I ask what they are waiting for—the gift of his life.

As I expected, the response to this speech is mixed. Some of the sachems, noticeably moved, nod their approval. Most of the bucks grunt no. Many believe that "Bahd-lar" has suffered enough and the dignity of the Shawanese has been preserved. After some wrangling, I ask that the vote be taken again. Everyone in the lodge, some 60 or 80 men, goes silent. I watch a wisp of smoke rising from one of the pipes, its cottony length curling slowly, holding shape in the thick still air. I can hear a dog barking somewhere outside. Light from the smoke-hole makes a plaque of jagged brightness on the earthen floor, and a fly is buzzing somewhere in the roof-poles. Then someone begins passing the tally stick from man to man around the walls. Throwing it to the ground is death. Passing it on means freedom. One old man, the skin on his face the color of dried tobacco and thin as parchment, acts as scorekeeper, recording each vote with a scrawl in the dust. When the counting is over, the scrawls are nearly evenly divided, but this time he is voted free.

Saving His Bacon
a Second Time:

the six of us unseen
when up the ravine he gallops
so close I can see
the beads on his moccasin
and Black Hoof, taking aim,
crooks his index finger
round the trigger guard,

the back of my hand
staying the hammer flint
which will strike the pan
ignite the powder
and force the pellet
through its tubular sheath
into Kenton's chest,

the general intent being
to disrupt cells
and throw the organism
into anarchy
sufficient to impair
or destroy
its ability to function.

Instead, we stand dumb
as beast and rider,
six legs, four eyes,
two manes, one tail
shrink into my thumbnail,
dissolve in the maples.

This is called
paying a debt with interest.

Simon (Butler) Kenton: An Interview

Kenton: "He was good to me. When he came up to me, when the Ingins had painted me black, I knew him at first. He asked me a good many questions, but I thought it was best not to be too for' ard, and I held back from telling him my name; but, when I did tell—oh! he was mighty glad to see me. He flung his arms round me, and cried like a child. I never did see one man so glad to see another yet. He made a speech to the Ingins—he could speak the Ingin tongue … and told them if they meant to do him a favor they must do it now, and save my life. Girty, afterwards, when we were at Detroit together, cried to me like a child, often, and told me he was sorry for the part he took against the whites; that he was too hasty. Yes, I tell you, Girty was good to me."

F. W. Thomas: "It's a wonder he was good to you."

Kenton: "No," he replied, quickly but solemnly, "It's no wonder. When we see our fellow creatures every day, we don't care for them; but it is different when you meet a man all alone in the woods—the wild lonely woods. I tell you, stranger, Girty and I met [here Kenton referred to a former meeting, before the Revolution and apparently when he and Girty had first become well acquainted], lonely men, on the banks of the Ohio, and where Cincinnati now stands, and we pledged ourselves one to the other, hand in hand, for life and death, when there was nobody in the wilderness *but God and us.*"

ON THE
OHIO

The Cabin

I DO NOT DISCOVER THE CABIN till I enter the square of its shade I am so intent on which path the turkey took, my dinner. A maze of buckthorn and blackberry brambles have nearly reclaimed what once was a clearing, snuffing out whatever was green and lower. Honeysuckle and grapevines, some larger than a man's thigh, run snarly up the slanting roof. Yellow moss on the shingles, each one carefully rived from white oak, stacked carefully as shields against the seasons, still sound. Unlike most cabins in the Territory, this one was built permanent, not just thrown together to satisfy the land office requirements for a homestead claim. More, that is, than the token four-square log pen and three rows of trifling corn among the stumps. But this one soundly built, put together with care, with skill. For one, there is a stone foundation, each stone as it came from the field carefully laid according to its size and shape to offer the best resistance to whatever it is that tugs up-things down. No mortar. None really needed. Not only the sills laid well but the logs themselves, great cuts of walnut and yellow poplar. And each log artfully hewn, squared with an adze, not roughed out, notched, and barked. The chinking is packed with mud and clay, maybe horsehair. No cat-and-clay chimney, but more masonry, choice flat white fieldstone stacked high and blocked, tapered gently toward the top. Corbels on it.

The door, which opens on the south, has two iron hinges (these must come 300 miles), the entrance clogged with rotting leaves which are strewn across the puncheon floor carelessly like so many dropped gloves. As I step over the threshold, I flush a sparrow from the loft. Startled, it flits around the rafters and bumps against three walls before I can step aside, as it wings past the door-jamb and away. Watching its frenzy, I see our small barn at Chambers' Mill, remembering the time my father, drunk beyond recall, armed my brothers and me with broombats to swat the sparrows which roosted among the roof-beams. And Thomas, scarcely walking he was so young, banging our only dish with a wooden spoon to stir them, dead sparrows littering the earthern floor. Nuisance, my father saying, nuisance. Hating anything English, except maybe Mother, even in name. Like the Indian-killer Whitley in Kentucky who raced horses round his track counter-clockwise because the English run them with the clock.

The one room, 10 by 10, loft and corners bare, naked pegs spaced along the rear wall. Yet it is not empty, being alive with presences. In one corner, a tilting stool is favoring its broken leg. There is a large iron stewpot rusting on its trivet by the hearth. Ashes, a half-burnt log. The only movement in the room is an oblong of orange light filtering through the oilskin flap which shivers in the wind. Too far for glass. In the chinking of the chimney, a mud dauber's nest, the long cylinders of dried white clay perforated at the ends. These vacant. Below, on the mantle, are several dead horse-flies, frail laced wings shriveled, their undersides a skein of tiny black bent wires, still glossed that patina of purple-green, last movements recorded in the dust.

Now I find my forefinger smearing my own name bold and definite in the blond furze. Puzzling out the only word I know to spell. S-I-M-O-N-G-I-R-T-Y. Each letter making a shallow moat. Leaving, I feel as if I'm still inside this place, there in the letters that spell my name, the sounds that signify the sound I answer to. Somehow held in the dust of that forsaken place, as if staring into a looking glass my image sticks to the frame though the substance has stepped beyond. Dauber, Housefly. Sparrow.

The Ohio River Valley

THE OHIO RIVER VALLEY: 200,111 square miles. Or France doubled. A larger portion of fertile, well-drained land than any other temperate region on the planet. Bordered on the east by a range of mountains; on the north by the Great Lakes; on the south and west by rivers; and twining through its heartland is another river. La Salle, the first recorded white to explore it, called it La Belle Riviere. The Shawnees named it Kist-ke-pi-la-sepe (Eagle River), or Youghiogheny (The River of Many White Caps). The English clip this to Ohio.

The Middle Ground is mantled by a dense forest of mixed hardwoods. Oak, ash, black and yellow walnut, wild cherry, coffee tree, honey and black locust, buck-eye, beech, shagbark hickory, hackberry, tulip poplar. Understories of dogwood, red bud, hawthorn, magnolia, and pawpaw. Some red cedar and hemlock, some pine. Timber so thick you can walk almost from one end to the other without stepping from shade. Parts of it grass or caneland, the best translation of Cantuckee being "the great meadow." Growing in this meadowland is bluegrass, pepper-grass, Virginia rye, wild ginger, pea vine, red clover, and Shawnee cabbage. One part, "the Barrens," is periodically burned by the Indians to attract elk and buffalo which graze in great herds, following deep roads or traces between the springs ticking the countryside. One of them, Big Bone Lick, has the largest and most plentiful specimens of prehistoric mammals found on the continent. Relics of the Ice

Age. Mammoths, mastodons, peccaries, tapirs, primitive horses, and prehistoric elk. The richest soil lies on a plateau of Ordovician limestone called the Cincinnati Arch, the oldest real estate in North America.

Wildlife is abundant. Buffalo, wapiti [the American elk), Virginia white-tail deer, wildcats, yellow wolf, black and gray fox, panthers, raccoons, black, gray, striped, and fox squirrels, red flying squirrels, pole cats, beavers, black bears, mink. Wild turkeys, pheasants, partridges, Carolina paroquets, ruffed grouse. The sun eclipsed for hours by passenger pigeons.

> In the fall of the year 1790, after the famine, beech mast abounded in the forest on the bottom lands, which brought in the turkeys in such countless numbers, that the inhabitants were obliged to gather their corn before it was fully ripe to save it from their ravages; and to cover their stacks of grain with brush. One man killed forty in a day with his rifle. They were caught in pens, killed with clubs and dogs by the boys, until a turkey would not sell for six cents, the people being cloyed, like the Israelites with quails. They were very fat; and full grown ones weighed from sixteen to thirty pounds.
>
> —*Pioneer History*

The water stirring with fish. Catfish, sunfish, spotted perch, mullet, chubs, and long-nosed gar. Bass and crappie, freshwater clams.

The black cat and the pike were the largest among the aquatic races. The yellow cat, white perch, salmon, spotted perch, sturgeon, and buffalo, were all fine fish, weighing from five to fifty pounds. A black cat was caught by James Patterson, a professed fisherman, in 1790, which weighed ninety-six pounds. He anchored his canoe at the mouth of the Muskingum, just at dark, threw out his lines, and wrapping himself in his blanket, lay down in the boat for a nap of sleep. This fish got fast to one of his hooks, and had strength to drag the canoe and light stone anchor from the edge of the shoal into deep water, and then float down to near the head of the island, where he found himself on awaking.

—*Pioneer History*

The heartland has a humid continental climate with marked differences between winter and summer, the mean annual temperature being about 54 degrees F. Winters are relatively mild, the average temperature ranging from 31 to 35 degrees during the coldest months. The temperature seldom drops below 0 degrees or rises beyond 100. Half of the year is frost-free, the last killing frost occurring around April 20th and the first around October 20th. Annual rainfall varies from 40 to 50 inches and is usually distributed to provide adequate rain during the growing season, although some portions often flood during the spring and suffer drought for several weeks during the summer.

Aborigines in 1750: 25,000 to 30,000 North American Indians. Five to six thousand warriors. Woodland peoples— divided into tribes and clans within tribes. The Delawares, for instance, consist of three main clans—the Unamis (Turtle), the Unalachtgo (Turkey), and the Monsey or Minsi (Wolf). They live in towns and villages along the waterways. Although corn and squash are grown among some of them, these tribes subsist as hunters and gatherers.

The tribes living east of the Mississippi consist of three great families, or parent tribes, the separate branches having dissimilar languages but all derived from the original family stock. Largest of these, the Algonquin, whose tribes extend from Hudson Bay on the east to the Mississippi and Lake Winnipeg on the west. Numbering a fourth or possibly a third of the entire Indian population, they include almost all of the New England tribes, the tribes centering around the Great Lakes, and those in the Northwest Territory, including Virginia and Kentucky.

The Iroquois (Algonquin for "real adders"), the second great family, occupy the eastern center of the Algonquin domain, an island in a vast sea. The Wyandots, Andastes, and Eries (Cat People), as well as the Cherokees to the south, are of Iroquois stock. The third family, located south of the Algonquins in the Gulf states, are known as Kuskhogean or Appalachians. They form a loose confederacy of Creeks, Choctaws, Chickasaws, Seminoles, and a number of lesser tribes within the same boundaries. There is overlapping, of course, and each family occupies or hunts portions of The Middle Ground.

The Iroquois, who call themselves Acmanoschioni (literally "one house, one fire, one canoe," or The United People), are also known as The Six Nations. They comprise a league or confederacy made up of the following tribes:

1. Sankhícani (The Fire-Striking People), or Mohawks, from "Sankhican" meaning gunlock, this tribe being the first to be given muskets by the Europeans. The flash which the locks

made when the musket was fired astonished their neighbors and gave them their name.

2. W'Tássone (The Stone-Pipe Makers), or Oneidas. The Oneidas were renowned for the manufacture of stone pipes for smoking tobacco.

3. Onondágoes, Onondagas (On-the-Top-of-the-Hill People), a reference to the site of their town.

4. Quéugue, or Cayugas (Lake People) named for the lake on which they lived of the same name.

5. Maechachtínni (Mountaineers or Great Hill People), or Senecas, from Ge-nun-de-wah-gauh, the mountain at the head of Lake Canandaigua sacred to them as their birthplace and council-site. According to their beliefs, their history begins when they broke forth from the earth at the top of the mountain.

6. Tuscaroras (Hemp Gatherers) from the great use they made of Apocynum Cannabinim. They were a late addition to the confederacy and were not recognized by the Delawares, who described the Iroquois as containing five nations instead of six.

Other tribes prominent in The Middle Ground are Wyandots (Dwellers on the Island), known also as Hurons (from the French huré, "rough") and as Loups (wolves); Miamis (People of the Pigeons); Delawares (from the river where they lived originally, named for Lord De La Warr, second governor of Virginia), known among themselves as Lenni Lenape (variously translated as People of the Rising Sun, Eastlanders, The Real People, or True Men); Shawnees, Shawano, Shawanese, or Oshawano (People of the South), the Weas, or Twightwees (The Cry of the Loon, associated with the river in western Indiana on which they lived);

Mingoes ("stealthy" or "treacherous"), a hodge-podge of misfits and renegades from all the tribes, but chiefly the Cayugas and Senecas; Potawatomies (People of the Place of the Fire, or simply Fire Nation); Kaskaskias, Illinois (The Lake of Men); and Peorias.

These tribes live north of the Ohio and mostly along rivers that drain into it: the Great Miami (Oswene, Delaware for Stone Creek), the Little Miami (Pioquonee, Delaware for High-Bank River), the Scioto (Elk River, or from seeyo toh, "Great Legs," a reference to the great number of its branches), the Wabash, the Muskingum (Musking-cepe, Delaware for Goose Creek), and the Hockhocking (from Hock-hock-uk, "bottle river"). Cherokees (People of a Different Speech) and Chickasaws live to the south of the Ohio. Far south, for no Indians live in Cantuckee, the ground being reserved for hunting and fighting.

Excluding the Chippewas, the most accurate breakdown, of warriors which could be assembled on the frontier at the time of the Revolution was made by Col. George Morgan of Ft. Pitt:

THE SIX NATIONS CONSIST OF

Mohawks	100
Oneidas and Tuscarawas	400
Cuyahogas	220
Onondagas	230
Senecas	650
	———
TOTAL	1,600
Delawares and Munsies	600
Shawanees of Scioto	400
Wyandots of Sandusky and Detroit	300

Ottawas, of Detroit and Lake Michigan	600
Chippewas, of all the lakes, said to be	5,000
Pottewatemies, of Detroit and Lake Michigan	400
Pyankeshas, Kickapoos, Muscoutans, Vermillions, Weotonans, &. c., on the Ouabache	800
TOTAL	8,100

White population in 1750: a few hundred French, a few hundred British. Mostly soldiers. A fair number of trappers and traders, some priests.

In 1749 the Marquis De la Galissoniere, commandant general of New France, directed Captain Celeron de Bienville and three hundred men to travel the country and take formal possession of the discoveries made by La Salle on the Ohio and its tributaries as far as the Appalachian mountains. Starting at Detroit, Celeron journeyed from Presque Isle down the Allegheny to the Ohio and downstream to its junction with the Mississippi. In order to perfect French claims, he was instructed to erect a wooden cross and bury a leaden plaque at the mouth of the principal rivers that fall into the Ohio.

In the spring of 1798, nearly fifty years later, flood-waters at the mouth of the Muskingum ate away much of its banks. That summer some boys who were swimming there found a square metallic plate projecting from the embankment three or four feet below the earth's surface. Prying it loose with a pole, they found it to be lead engraved with letters from some unknown tongue. Not thinking it of any value, they took it home where chunks of it were cut up and molded into rifle balls. Which, at the time, were scarce and valuable.

News of the discovery came to a Paul Fearing, Esq., who got possession of the plate, its message now less than complete, and had it translated. Eventually, the plate was sent to DeWitt Clinton, governor of New York, who gave it to the Antiquarian Society of Massachusetts in 1827.

In March of 1847, a similar plate was found at the mouth of the Kanawha. Eleven by seven inches and from one-eighth to one-fourth inch thick, with the engraver's name, Paul Le Brosse, on the back, the tablet read:

LAN, 1749, DV DEGNE DE LOVIS XV ROY DE FRANCE, NOVS CELORON, COMMANDANT DVN DETACHEMENT ENVOIE PAR MONSIEVR LE MS. DE LA GALISSONIERE, COMMANDANT GENERAL DE LA NOVVELLE FRANCE, POVR RETABLIR LA TRANQVILLITE DANS QVELQVES VILLAGES SAUVAGES DE CES, CANTONS AVONS ENTERRE CETTE PLAQVE A LENTREE DE LA RIVIERE CHINODAHICHETHA, LE 18 AOUST. PRES DE LA RIVIERE OYO, AUTREMENT BELLE RIVIERE, POVR MONVMENT DV RENOVVELLEMENT DE POSSESSION, QVE NOVS AVONS PRIS DE LA DITTE RIVIERE OYO, ET DE TOVTES CELLES QVI Y TOMB'NT, ET DE TOVES LES TERRES DES DEVX COTES JVSQVE AVX SOVRCES DES DITTES RI-VIES, AINSI QVEL ONT JOVY 0V DV JOVIR LES PRECEDENTS ROYS DE FRANCE, ET QVILS SI-SONT MAINTENVS PAR LES ARMES, ET PAR LES TRAITTES, SPECIALEMENT PAR

CEVX DE RISV-VICK DUTRCHT ET DAIX LA
CHAPELLE.

The translation was made by L. Soyer, Esq., mayor of Marietta, Ohio, a person skilled in the French language, himself a native of France:

> In the year 1749, of the reign of Louis XV, of France, We, Celoron, commandant of a detachment sent by the Marquis de la Galissoniere, Captain-General of New France, in order to re-establish tranquility among some villages of savages of these parts, have buried this plate at the mouth of the river Chi-no-da-hich-e-tha, the 18th August, near the river Ohio, otherwise beautiful river, as a monument of renewal of possession, which we have taken of the said river Ohio, and of all those which empty themselves into it, and of all the lands of both sides, even to the sources of said rivers; as have enjoyed, or ought to have enjoyed the preceding kings of France, and that they have maintained themselves there, by force of arms and by treaties, especially by those of Riswick, of Utrecht, and of Aix-la-Chapelle.

These plates are act and prelude to the French and Indian War. The Shawanese have a myth to explain their origin and the presence of white men in the New World. God was an Indian, the myth tells us. As Master of Life he made the Shawanese before any other race. As they sprang from his brain, he gave them what knowledge he himself possessed and set them on a great island (America). All the other families and tribes of red men descended from the Shawanese, who became everyone's grandfather. The Creator then went on to lesser tasks. He made the French and English out of his breast, the Dutch out of his feet, and the Long Knives (Americans) out of his hands. These inferior races he placed in another land beyond the Atlantic, which was known to his children as the "stinking lake."

ROGERS
(The War)

Ambush on the River, 1779

WE DON'T SPY DAVID ROGERS'
KEELBOATS SOONER because the
river bends at this point. Which is about 3
miles below the Little Miami at the mouth of the Licking. "We"
is a menagerie of Senecas, Wyandots, Delawares, and Piqua Town
Shawnees, maybe 50 all told. As soon as we spot the boats, we
take tree, careful that no accidental noise or glint from our metal
should betray us. Only half of us are in a position to fight. The rest,
those with Brother George and Matt Elliot, are camped a quarter
mile upriver, having just rendezvoused from a hunt and preparing
to feast. They will be bait.

Fortunate for us, Rogers' party has crossed to our side of the
river. They do this in order to swallow the shank of the bend and
save the crew some water. A mistake. As they come into view, we
see both decks are loaded with men poling the shallows to make
headway against the currents, which are tricky at this spot. Maybe
70 in all. A line on either side of the cabins walks the length of the
boats, each man thrusting his weight against a pole. They are close,
so close I can hear their grunts and thump-thump of the poles
against the gunwales. And they have not seen us.

Then someone in the lead boat—who knows? maybe Rogers
himself—gets wind that George and his party are camped on the
sandbar around the bend. And Rogers cannot resist the temptation
to take them by surprise. Quickly, quietly, they beach the boats

and make for the bar, snaking through a patch of scraggly willows toward the camp, already counting the scalps, still ignorant that we are counting the bug-bites on their arses a few rods away. The wind has died down and it is dead quiet. The only sounds are the lapping of water and the scree of a few looping birds by the river. We wait while they crawl deeper into our trap.

My heart by this time is a mallet against my ribs. I feel the sweat liberal on my face and back, little spidery runnels streaming from my forehead, my mouth dry as cotton. I am so twitchy I feel I'll die if I don't make water. There is an itching back of my head. Moments pass and I can't hold off any longer. My first shot, the signal to attack, misfires. The powder stings my cheeks and smells of burnt hair. Later, someone will show me the splash of blue powder on my cheek, delicately formed in the pattern of a flower. I watch as Rogers' crewmen, caught off guard, scatter in panic, those that do not fall. Those left after our first fire make for some driftwood piled along the beach, scurrying across the sand like beetles from under a raised log.

Our first volley thins them considerably and brings on a rout, blue chuffs of smoke and the yells from Elliot's hunters, aroused now, bewildering the survivors, who bob from tree to tree, firing aimlessly in all directions. Cut off from the boats, they take what cover they can as both my braves and Elliot's drop their smoking rifles and tear into them for a scalping party. By this time I am loaded again. My second shot, cooler this time, downs Rogers. Hit in mid-stride, he crumples in a ball, collapses, just as I fire, I hear, almost see, a metal eye whiz past my ear. The air it displaces fans back past my eyebrow, tickling. I do not hear it, but I know I am laughing.

Some minutes pass and more of Rogers' men have fallen than are standing. A few are only nicked, but more are dead or dying. The five men he left with the boats put off in the smaller when the shooting starts. The larger boat, loaded to the gunwales and listing, is already ours. The stranded survivors, no more than 20 or so now, realize their peril and with enviable coolness fight their way to cover in the woods. Half my Wyandots pursue them. Half return to claim the spoils from the boat. One, a halfbreed named Knows-Too-Well, a bandy-legged dwarf of a man with dirty habits, prowls among the wounded, finishing them with a fishing spear. He's taken a handful of scalps as trophies; six powder horns are dangling from his neck. Our surprise is complete. Never have I seen so many dead in so short a time. The corpses lie thick as stumps across the sand, a field of broken pumpkins. The harvest is 42 dead and 5 taken prisoner. Our loss is 2 killed and 3 slightly wounded.

To our great joy, the boats are loaded with military stores bound for Virginia to fit out the militia. One of the prisoners, a stripling more boy than man, tells us Rogers was commissioned to purchase the supplies in New Orleans—dry goods, rum, fusees. Every square foot of the cabins is packed with bundles and boxes. This is what we find:

400	Match Coats. large & small
24	Pieces Strouds, blue
1,000	Shirts assorted, white ruffled, Callico ruffled, plain white & Checkd
200	French Rifles
8	C lb wt Powder
1,600	lb. Lead

40	Saddles
100	Bridles
50	Brass Kettles
60	Tin Kettles or rolld Iron
40	doz Cutteaus
4	doz Black silk Handkerchiefs
30	Regimental Coats, good
30	do Hats. half Silver laced good
4	doz Pewter Plates
1	doz Tea Kettles
1	Grs. Pewter spoons
2,000	Flints
100	dandruff Combs
4	doz Razors
200	lb Coffee
6	Bushels Salt
30	lb Bohea Tea
50	pair Yarn Mittens
50	worster Caps
6	doz Knives & Forks
60	pr Shoes & Buckles, 10 prs of them Silver
40	pr Spurs
20	pr White Linnen Breeches
10	pr Boots, large
12	pr Saddle Bags, black & red a compleat Set of Carpenters Tools a Set Coopers Tools
1,000	Fish Hooks large & small
1	Gro. brass Buttins

There is enough here to stake a dozen traders, enough hardware to buy a dozen tribes. This is not counting the kits and arms removed from the bodies. There are also 7 barrels of rum which I take into my personal custody. One I give the Indians for a celebration. The rest I store with my belongings. When the party starts, I reward myself with a dram or two and the pleasure of firing the fine brace of French pistols, smooth-bored with silver inlay, which I lift from Rogers' body.

The Narrative of Capt. Robert Benham

WHEN WE WERE TURNED FROM THE BOATS, I knew it was break the ring or perish. Root, hog, or die. Banding together, the fifteen or so of us with breath still in our bodies fired a last volley and rushed toward what seemed the weakest link in the ring. The savages, firing and darting among the trees, simply dispersed, fading deeper into the woods. Just as we broke through, I felt a keen, stabbing sensation somewhere below the waist. I had taken a ball which passed through my hams like a hot needle through wax. The impact pitched me to the ground near a fallen tree. This tree, a gigantic oak nearly five feet in diameter, had been struck by lightning nearly halfway up the trunk, the bulk of its branches forming a thick canopy.

And it was here, inch by inch, that I dragged myself, each motion exciting the most unbearable pain, a hurt which suffused itself throughout my body and which graduated from burning and throbbing to a persistent ache so intense it finally numbed my senses. Panting under the limbs, burrowing in the yellowed leaves, hearing the rifle shots as their thunder slowly spent itself, diminishing into random reports, finally ceasing. All the while imagining the arc of the hatchet which strikes the gully in my brain.

I am only half-conscious as the blurred forms streak past in pursuit of the others. Atom by atom I concentrate on melting my bulk in the shadows, now mercifully longer, certain that some portion of my naked self will expose me. At midnight I am still alive. There is no moon, only the chattering of crickets and cicadas, the white feel of night eyes beneath the insect sounds. The yelping has ceased and the woods have settled into a kind of steady fidget, that restless scratching below the surface of long summer nights. The pain in my legs has steadied to a blunt staccato. Fortunately, the bleeding has stopped, but my thighs are swollen to the girth of logs, and as heavy. I cannot wiggle my toes. Feeling a need to relieve myself, I cannot contrive a means to clear my person. Unable to move, I feel the urine trickle down my leg, soaking through my leather, warm and somehow soothing.

At dawn they return to strip the dead and gather booty from the remaining boat. The battlefield, what I can see of it, is strewn with corpses, bodies contorted in grotesque postures; some frozen in sleep, others with gaping mouths, all mutilated beyond recognition. For some reason I think of my father's orchard in Allentown and the combination of freezing rain and late snow which weighted and split the limbs, twisting and stunting the branches in hideous shapes, every tree. That spring the buds were blisters, leafless, diseased. The limbs that year and for years after bore tainted fruit.

The savages are leaving now. Several stragglers trot past my tree burdened with bundles of ready-made clothing plundered from the boat. One is wearing a braided officer's jacket, which looks ludicrous above his naked legs. The pain is so intense and my hunger so great I am almost tempted to signal them and trust to their mercy. I have not eaten in nearly twenty-four hours. I am utterly fatigued. My mind is alive with images of wolves devouring me after the savages have departed. In a few moments, the last Indian is out of sight and the woods are quiet again. I feel the dampness in the ground rise into my limbs until its wetness is a part of me, and I imagine myself shredding apart bit by bit into the mould.

Towards evening of this second day I hear a commotion, a scrambling, scratching sound in a tree nearby. A raccoon so close I can count the rings on his tail coming headfirst down a sugar tree, the eyes behind his bandit mask taking me for dead. I can taste him, the sweet greasy meat imparting strength to my battered limbs. Carefully I draw up my musket, which fortunately I was able to drag to my hiding place. I steady the heavy barrel in the fork of a limb and trip the trigger. Down he tumbles and lands motionless only twenty paces away, but alas, much farther than I can crawl. Just after I fire, I hear a cry somewhere off to my right. Certain that I have been discovered, I reload frantically and prepare for the worst. Soon I hear another cry, this time nearer. With my thumb I draw back the hammer until it locks, and wait. A third time this voice halloos, but in this instance adding impatiently, "Whoever you are, for God's sake, answer me." Certain now that the voice belongs to no Indian, I make my own feeble reply, and this is the means by which Nicholas Bruner and I make our union.

While both of my hips have been shattered, rendering me a cripple, Bruner has lost the use of his arms, both of them fractured below the elbow. Wounded during the fray, he too took cover and had been overlooked in the confusion. I pointed him to the raccoon, which he retrieved with a series of kicks. Having the use of my hands, I cleaned and dressed it, roasting it over a small fire whose kindling he raked up with his feet. I fed him with my own hands, and after we had both eaten our fill, plastered his arms with mud and fashioned crude splints for us both. How to convey water was a problem until he devised a means of using my hat as a bucket by clamping the brim in his teeth. Wading neck-high into the Licking, he dunked his head, thus filling the hat. Taking great pains not to spill any, he would then fetch it to me with his teeth.

For several weeks we lived in this manner while our wounds healed. When the game near about was exhausted, we hobbled to another site where we built a lean-to to keep us from the elements. Gradually, we worked our way downriver. Once we stumbled over some grouse, which made an excellent dinner. One night we slept in a hollow sycamore, a tree so large it would accommodate us both very comfortably. Another time we met with an Indian dog and killed it, but the meat was so poor we could not eat it. Bruner put it on the fire and baked it, but a little of the blood made him sick. He found some ground cherries too, but they did not agree with him either. Though rabbits and squirrels were scarce, the woods abounded with fat gobblers which he would shoo into my sights, turkeys being the stupidest of all fowl, their dull wits compensated for only by their succulence.

Slowly recovering our strength, we retraced our steps along the Licking to the Ohio where we hoped to flag a boat which would take us to the Falls and safety. On the morning of the 27th, a full six weeks after the ambush, Bruner spotted a flatboat leisurely floating down the river. Hoisting my hat on a stick, I shouted and waved to attract their notice. When they continued to drift downstream despite our efforts to hail them, we were certain they were infirm as we, being both deaf and blind. But when they were almost out of sight, a small canoe put off and cautiously approached our side of the river. After giving our names and circumstances and answering a dozen particulars about our families and acquaintances, we persuaded them to come to shore and take us aboard. At first, believing us to be savages, decoys at least, they had steered for the opposite side of the river. As it was, we were spectres of our former selves. I limping on makeshift crutches, poor Bruner in his slings, both nearly naked as the day we entered Creation, cheeks and chins briared with six weeks' beard, alive.

Ft. Laurens

THIS TIME THERE ARE 120 OF US, Wyandots and Mingoes, not counting 10 British commanded by Capt. Henry Byrd. The Mingoes are mine, made up entirely of Senecas, some I have known since Cattaraugus. The Wyandots are under Byrd and not happy about it. There would have been more, maybe five or six hundred, were they under someone they trusted. This Byrd is a newcomer, a spiny young captain from the King's Regiment [the 8th) who volunteered to come along to see "how well the Indians behave." Fussy and a trifle stiff in his scarlet coat, his brass buttons and sword, he gets off wrong with the Wyandots, who sense in him a softness which they scorn.

There was also an incident. When Byrd came to Sandusky from Detroit, he found the Wyandots amusing themselves with a prisoner. Stupidly, he tried to spoil their sport, offering them $400 for the American's life and otherwise making a fool of himself. The prisoner, lone survivor of a flatboat ambushed on the Ohio, thanked him for his trouble, then turned to condemn Bad Shoes and the other Wyandots. He said the time will come when they would pay dearly for their murders. Which it probably will. With that, he was marched off and tortured to death at a slow rate. When the Wyandots were satisfied he was dead, Byrd recovered the body and buried it, but it was dug up again and the head placed on a pole. So Byrd took it down and buried it again, this time secretly. When they came around looking for it, he denounced them as cowards.

He called them damned rascals and devils, brave only when they could cut on innocent prisoners in the safety of their village, and other such compliments. The Wyandots, to say the least, were displeased with him. A few wanted to put a knife in his back. More to their liking were the arms and ammunition he brought from Detroit.

Which brings us to Ft. Laurens. The man in command was Col. John Gibson, a messmate from Dunmore days, the same John Gibson who wrote out the speech I delivered from Logan after Point Pleasant. A few days ago, one of his couriers was killed near Ft. McIntosh. Among the papers he was carrying was a letter in which he boasted to Gen. McIntosh that should I fall into his hands he would take the keenest pleasure in "trepanning" me. When Byrd explained this to me, I vowed to return the favor.

The fort itself was small, covering less than an acre, but strongly made. It stood on the west bank of the Tuscarawas below the mouth of Sandy Creek. It was the farthest west of any fort the Americans had yet raised. It was also the first "permanent" fort to be erected in the Ohio country. Though the garrison was small, not numbering over a hundred men, it was an affront to the Wyandots, an insult to their dignity. And naturally they reacted. One cannot kick the nest without expecting the yellowjackets to swarm.

Now the ruse. Or ruses. The horses kept at the fort were permitted to forage on patches of prairie grass outside the walls. To keep them from straying, bells were placed around their necks so they could be located easily. Arriving outside the fort undetected, we rounded up the horses and slipped just out of sight of the stockade, but not out of hearing. Then we hid ourselves in clumps of tall grass and waited.

As expected, a party was sent out to investigate. Toward noon 16 men filed out around a mule-drawn wagon. They moved in the direction of the tinkling bells. Toward us, that is. Some of them were carrying axes, so we knew they meant to cut firewood as well as gather the strays. By the time they had moved a quarter mile from the fort, they were well within the corridor we formed for them. When several put down their rifles and took up axes to chop some windfalls, Byrd gave the signal with his sword. The next instant one hundred and twenty-odd rifle shots walloped the calm like a thunder-clap, shattering it with a hundred tiny death-beads. The ground under our feet shook for an instant, then steadied. We were so close 14 fell on the first volley. The wagoner, somehow uninjured, tried to mount the surviving mule and make it back to the fort. He and one of the soldiers were taken prisoner, so our tally was complete. Next came the scalping, which didn't really interest me. After a few minutes, Bad Shoes returned from the wagon grinning, two fresh scalps hanging from his belt. Not one of ours was even scratched, and everyone, even Byrd for once, was gloating. Plan Number One came off neat as you please.

The fort, of course, was alerted then, and we drew up around it for a siege. Scheme Number Two was to deceive Gibson, who had boasted in his letter that he would defend the fort "to the last extremity." The plan was to make him believe he was outnumbered. To accomplish this, the Wyandots and Mingoes put on a masquerade. They painted and costumed themselves in a grand manner to stage a show of force in the woods around the fort, careful the while to keep out of rifle range. They made fancy maneuvers and counter-marches at several points around the stockade to give the impression that we were several times our number. When we asked for a parley, Gibson refused. So there would be no misunderstandings, he directed a shot at Bad Shoes, who was waving a strip of white linen from his rifle. Which missed.

This failing, we decided to wait them out. When targets appeared, we fired at them. But mainly our strategy was to starve or freeze them into surrender. And we almost succeeded. Months after the siege was lifted, we learned that rations during the final days were reduced to a quarter pound of sour flour and an equal weight of spoiled meat per day. Desperate for fuel, they dismantled some of the cabins for firewood. They approached, in a word, Gibson's "last extremity."

But luck was with them. Twenty-five days we waited them out. At the end of that time, Byrd and I could no longer restrain our homesick Indians. They had dealt a blow to the Mechanschican, the Long Knives. Good. They had taken some scalps. Better. But the siege had fizzled. When scouts reported that a large relief force was approaching from Ft. McIntosh, we simply faded into the woods and marched back to Sandusky.

Big Bone Lick

I feel the bones of great beasts
sucking through the ooze,
the furry souls of mammoths
terraced in the muck,
tongues of jealous fossils
itching for my salt.

Among the bone-herds
poking from the marsh
are 10-pound teeth and tapir skulls,
tusks of arctic elephants
curved gracefully as swans.

I stretch my tent
on borrowed ribs,
I bunk on ivory spines.
My sleep is strung with broken pearls,
trapped mammals sticky
in my dreams,
extinction and the Age of Ice
nudging at my meat.

November 1, 1779: First Snow

A sense of beginnings.
The light more intense.
Sound furred in deep shawls.
The slopes purified of all detail.
The snow made literate with my feet.

The Hard Winter

The Hard Winter of '79
snow rose to our waists
before it froze
Rivers lockt hands
Creeks went crystal stiff
with diamond fish

Wind blew so chill
brutes sang in the woods
The maples split & crackt
like pistols
Frost bit green cane
& rain fell frigid needles

It turned so cold
tirkies tumbled off their roosts
& broke like china
Cows hugged chimneys
till the mucus
in their nostrils froze

I lost one toe

A Stirring of Leaves

S O M E T I M E S I would pass whole months solitary in the woods. No mammal company, neither horse nor dog. No bread, no sugar, no salt. No spirits. No woman. My life kept spare and simple. Saw no face, no creature that stalked on two legs. All four-leggeds. Nor heard sound of human voice but mine. The closest I came to my own kind being a gunshot, the explosion one afternoon prying into my silence, sliding slow thunder over the hills until I heard only the familiar stirring of leaves above my head. Company I shunned, not feeling social. Time to myself, slack. When I was hungry, I ate. When tired, slept. Sick, I drank root tea or chewed bitterroot. It being midsummer, game was easy, so place and direction meant little, though I shied from the licks and buffalo trails where I would likely meet hunters. The same with rivers with their camps and traffic.

I learn to be social with myself, my own company. To be easy with each of my several voices. The talking voice and the other, the sulky one mute as a persimmon. This second, though, is given to fancies, fat with visions, superstitious, a buck-eye wearing itself bald in its pocket, the one which won't pick watercress or eat Irish potatoes during Christmas. These voices argue the weather, what path to take, which tracks belong to which varmint, the complexion of the devil. Gradually I feel my body stretch beyond itself, my skin take form in roots or currents, hard or liquid. I come into the mystery of trees, come to see their textures and moods as mirrors of my own, each leaf hungry for its rill of light, pitching its lump of shade, undersides curled in a cloudburst. The feel of just-cut wood, stringy white fibers, my fingers tracing the grains, the ribs of severed growth. I learn some alphabets: which woods burn best, wet or dry; how to follow a bee-line; the scantiest load of powder to pot a winging partridge; which herbs are tasty, which not. Which cures what. Got so I could feel rain days before it fell, know from scrabbles in the dust which bird had had its dust-bath. The habits of animals. For two weeks I had a pet raccoon till one day it bit my finger and, hurting, I killed it. Nights I take to whittling before the fire, starting with spoons and toy animals, then to bowls which I gouged from buckeye. When I finished, I left each where it lay, having no shelf.

For one cycle of the moon I camp in dense woods near a river which cuts a spectacular gorge. The creek I camp on is a feeder running on sheets of gray shale, the water a deep bottle-green. Its bed is flanked by sandstone blocks which have tumbled from the steep embankments, some chunks the size of cabins. The banks themselves are cut by currents, especially the brisk ones when it floods. The result is cobbles of white rocks paving the streambed and uprooted trees, the bleached roots cracked and twisted as if in pain. A few hold their grips in the slanting banks, defying the earth's pull, some thriving horizontal instead of up. Cottonwoods, birches, water, not sugar-maples, sycamores, a few wandering beeches, an understory of laurel and rhododendron, dogwood and sassafras making a canopy over my head, a thread of pale sky left between the topmost branches. So dense and high are these, the sun can be seen only an hour each side of noon, I walk a green furrow plowed deep in the earth's skin, my sky whittled thin by rock and leaf. In these narrows I am at home.

My feet make all my decisions. My choices are to hazard a footing over the rocks or wade along shallows in the creek. My feet choose the water, which is no deeper than my ankles in most places except for some falls where the turbulence has swirled and dug potholes. So my leather won't shrink, I unbind my moccasins and store them in my pack. The woods, my ears, fill with water sounds. Trickles, rushes, eddies, seepings flow through my head until they become familiar and so a part of my silence. The grade is easy. A man could march miles in this creek, the water cool and marbly on his feet, skin limp and blank over the blue veins, heels cushioned on sand and red gravel. And I do. All one day and part of the next, and still going.

Late afternoon of the second day the sky turns pewter and I scan for shelter against the storm I know is coming. A little farther and I spot a fist of rock jutting over the water. A kind of unfinished bridge. On a sandbar under this overhang I make camp. The sand makes a natural mattress, the overhang a natural roof. On the nether side I find black smudges that only smoke can make. So I know I am not the first here. Driftwood, barkless and seasoned for burning, is scattered over the beach. The place is perfect. So remote my smoke is lost in rhododendron before it rises high enough to see.

Days here take on a pattern. Waking at dawn, baking fish in my ashes or chewing jerked meat, sucking long cool draughts from the stream, making waste, airing my robes. The prime of day to fish, shoot, explore, or plain loaf. Loafing. I watch the minnows in my pool for hours as they needle in and out of the shade, feeding on what I cannot cipher in the leaf-murk of the bottom. And fed on by things bigger and fleeter—blue-gills, bass, even crawfish. Their silver backs, as they flit and turn, catch sun, which makes them vulnerable, light as that sky color which protects their undersides, only more flashy. Sometimes I sight the lone snapper, royalty on this snatch of creek, scrounging under sunk logs, his claw-feet raising clouds of yellow silt as he scuds along the bottom. His soundless, dream-like motion smooth and deadly, his passage released from sound, this world. Toe-crushing jaws. Sometimes, near noon, I see a fat drab watersnake stretched out on a rock or log, sapping sunlight.

One morning I follow a shite-poke nearly a mile upstream. When my eye finds his shape against the wood-line, he is poised on his perch, the stub of a broken limb. As I move closer, he flies. Wary of my human shape, which is new to him, hence deadly. From dead limb to dead limb he is pushed up the creek. Each time I cross an invisible line he drops from his perch, lifting and pumping his wide heron-wings on to the next. Does this maybe a dozen times as I move up the creek before he fixes a remedy. Suddenly he wheels in mid-flight, flapping rapidly back, fans back past my head toward his starting point, So close he scares me. So close I feel the air creased and rumpled by his wings. He passes out of my sight, but my mind knows he will settle again and wait, his long sword-like beak cocked and slanting toward water. For a fact there is no wind here. Each tree, each rock, seems wedded to its place, ancient. This stretch full of beards, thick with follicles of moss, swept silent with ferns. Only me and the water animate as I stop to watch. My feet, the only distortion in the clear rock detail of the bottom, the cool weaving through my toes.

Portrait of Thayendanegea

Thayendanegea, the name means
He-who-sets-two-bets-together,
an alias for Joseph Brant (1742–1807);
he is better known as Captain Brant
or plain Brant.
Leader of the Mohawks,
principal war-chief of the Six Nations;
brother-in-law to Sir William Johnson,
chief Indian agent for the Crown.

Educated by Eleazar Wheelcock, D.D.,
at what will become Dartmouth College
where he becomes a communicant
in the Anglican Church,
revises the Mohawk Prayer Book,
translates the Acts of the Apostles
and the Gospel of Mark into Mohawk.
During his visit to England
where Boswell and Romney paint his portrait,
he is entertained by the King and Queen.

His person was about six feet high,
was finely proportioned, stout and muscular;
his eyes large, bright, and piercing;

his forehead high and broad;
his nose aquiline;
his mouth rather wide;
and his countenance open and intelligent,
expressive of firmness and decision.

Siding with the Tories during the Revolution,
he fights at Cherry Valley,
the battles of Oriskany, Minisink
& Chemung,
the massacre at Wyoming
(where verse renders him immortal
as "Monster Brant" in Campbell's
"Gertrude of Wyoming"),
the destruction of German Flats,
the burning of Harpersfield,
the defeat of Lochry,
and the routing of St. Clair,
surviving the war
to die peacefully at 65
at his home on Lake Ontario,
his last words being,
"Have pity on the poor Indians."

Brant

BROTHER GEORGE GETS UP TO STIR THE FIRE. The rest of us are too drunk. Besides George, there is Brant, McKee, a Canadian ranger named Thompson, two or three of Brant's Mohawks, and myself. Why we are drunk: first, there is nothing else to do, camped as we are across the river watching for Clark to move his army out of Louisville where we can attack him. Also because we are celebrating. George and Brant have joined us after ambushing Col. Lochry and his Pennsylvanians. The ambush took place on the Ohio somewhere below the mouth of the Great Miami and 106 men were killed or taken. Lochry fell into a trap. Landing at an inlet and turning his horses ashore to graze, he was caught in a crossfire from the bluff and nearly annihilated. His men were roasting a buffalo, and the attack came so suddenly some died with meat in their mouths. All his stores—beef, blankets, powder, lead ingots, and a quantity of rum—came into our hands. The rum is almost drunk, the drinking having started late in the afternoon, the camp getting rowdier and rowdier as the Indians break up into separate parties to horse around, some whooping, dancing, and throwing their tomahawks, others lounging around the fires.

George, as I said, is least affected. Thompson is next. This Canadian is a slight man, small with quick ferret eyes. He has an odd habit of cocking his head to one side as if he hears sounds the rest of us don't. Not drinking much but drinking steady. Talks and misses little. I make a note not to trust him. George and McKee have drunk about the same, but you would not know it. Drink doesn't tell so much on George as McKee whose comments by this time make no sense to anyone. Drunk or sober, McKee is a mystery. There is something moony about him. Maybe this is because he acts with no plan, moves from one sensation to the next, his nerves like delicate springs on a trap triggered by the slightest impulse, steel jaws ready to clap on a footfall. The part he plays is written as he goes. His life, one long acting out of inconsistent parts no one can follow. One of the Mohawks has passed out, snoring steadily, one foot nearly in the fire. I've had my share. Forgetting to eat, I am in the altitudes again, feeling pranky and a little mean.

As for Brant, the rum has a purchase on his tongue. Since whipping Lochry his pride walks on all fours. It knows no bounds. Fat and liquid, he slides on his own oil. Only look at him. He wears a scarlet frock which is cut around his middle with a silken sash. Puke yellow. In one side, he has tucked Lochry's sword as a kind of trophy. It's a wonder he can walk for all the beads and trinkets he's wearing. Gold epaulets and silver bracelets, doodads. Tricked out like walking plunder, around his neck he wears a large medallion of his Sovereign Majesty George III. A keepsake. No one seems to listen as he exaggerates his own role in the fighting. How he did this and ordered that, masterminding the whole attack. George takes it all in, but does not mind being robbed of glory so long as he is not robbed of his share of loot. So Brant goes on to boast how he took 11 scalps which are stretched on hoops outside his lodge, one the rarest gold. A collector's item, he tells us. Goes on to brag how he fought with fangs of the adder, teeth of the bear, cunning of the fox, etc. When he claims he captured 8 prisoners single-handed, I make my mistake, call him liar.

Before I can raise my arm to ward the blow, he whips the sword from his waist and in one deft stroke comes down hard on my forehead.

When I wake, it is light. Which day or how long after I don't know. My eyes open on the sun-beat orange of canvas. Air stale and pregnant with my own smell. My tent covering me like a shroud. Flies are holding congress on my skull, their drones incessant, a thousand sticky tongues fast to the pastry on my forehead. I am a mess of pain and itchiness. A mess. My head is ragged fringe, a scramble of broken pictures and floating hurt. Pain digs a crooked trench in my skullbone and settles down to stay.

Days pass before I can rise higher than my elbow. The longest I've stayed in one place as long as I know. So long I am afraid my legs will forget walking. My head unaccustomed to roofs. For days I fester, pressed in the belly of a dismal black cloud. Just when I think I'll die if the discomfort doesn't leave, the healing takes. The skin stitches back, but slack and wrinkled like a raisin. Packed with a gummy poultice of bear oil and mud, the gash puckers into a scar. Pink as a cow's tongue. Not coarse like ordinary skin, it feels sickly smooth, silky. Lowering my face at the spring to suck in the cool, I see in reverse the pink trail slanting cross my forehead, the traveled pathway running north by northwest. A keepsake.

The Massacre at Gnadenhutten

It's so simple for dogs
who know just where
their territory ends,
the frontiers of smell,
boundaries of lick and bark.

But civilized and savage
the lines are not so clear:
On March 8th, 1782,
Col. Williamson with 100 volunteers
crosses the Tuscarawas River
at Gnadenhutten
(Cabins of Grace),
and captures 98 Moravian Indians
as they hoe their corn,
Christian converts.

Locking them in their mission,
he orders them executed
"to teach the Delawares a lesson."
>   35 men
>   27 women
>   34 boys

(2 boys escaping)

Capt. Charles Builderback
personally kills and scalps 14
staving their skulls with a mallet.

A Warning

DON'T SAY I DIDN'T WARN THEM.
Not that I have much use for Delawares who bury the
hatchet for skirts and Jesus. For months I pleaded with
Hamilton to move them somewhere safe, someplace, at least, where
they could do us no harm. Fact is, both sides saw them as go-
betweens, spies passing news to interested parties. And now this.
Alive, they were dangerous, bad examples. Dead, they are powder
in our fire, lessons to the tribes that lean toward peace. Most of
them parroted the missionaries, spoke English, sang hymns, called
their babies by Christian names, raised corn instead of scalps.
Went soft. So now they will join their fathers in wooden boxes
with Christian prayers spoken over them. Rabbits and turkeys are
made for stews, lambs made for slaughter.

Declension

Ningee chaw gie zo go,
Kegah chaw gie zo göm,
Tah chaw giz wah,
Kegah chaw gie zo go min,
Kegah chaw giz zo göm,
Tah chaw giz waw wug,
I shall be burned.
Thou shalt be burned.
He shall be burned.
We shall be burned.
Ye or you shall be burned.
They shall be burned.

Col. William Crawford (1732-1782)

A Virginian of the old cloth
before the breed forgot its Latin
and petered out,
swapping its promise for frills;
for rhetoric and horses.

A Revolutionary soldier,
lifelong friend of Washington,
summoned from retirement
to lead a punitive expedition
against the Indians in Ohio.

Taken during the retreat
from the Upper Sandusky
when he returned from safety
to hunt his son, his nephew,
and his son-in-law,
who were among the missing.

From "Account of the Capture and Torture of Col. William Crawford as reported by Dr. John Knight"

'**M**ONDAY MORNING, the 10th of June 1782, we were paraded to march to Sandusky, about thirty-three miles distant; they had eleven prisoners of us and four scalps, the Indians being seventeen in number.

"Col. Crawford was very desirous to see a certain Simon Girty, who lived with the Indians, and was on this account to go to town the same night, with two warriors to guard him, having orders at the same time to pass by the place where the Col. had turned out his horse, that they might if possible, find him. The rest of us were taken as far as the old town which was within eight miles of the new.

"Tuesday morning, the eleventh, Col. Crawford was brought out to us on purpose to be marched in with the other prisoners. I asked the Col. if he had seen Girty? He told me he had, and that Girty had promised to do every thing in his power for him, but that the Indians were very much enraged against the prisoners, particularly Captain Pipe one of the chiefs, he likewise told me that Girty had informed him that his son-in-law Col. Harrison and his nephew William Crawford, were made prisoners by the Shawanese but had been pardoned. This Capt. Pipe had come from the towns about an hour before Col. Crawford, and had painted all the prisoners' faces black.

"We were then conducted along toward the place where the Col. was afterward executed; when we came within about half a mile of it, Simon Girty met us, with several Indians on horseback; he spoke to the Col., but as I was about one hundred and fifty yards behind could not hear what passed between them.

"Almost every Indian we met struck us either with sticks or their fists. Girty waited until I was brought up and asked, was that the Doctor?—I told him yes, and went toward him reaching out my hand, but he bid me begone and called me a damned rascal, upon which the fellows who had me in charge pulled me along, Girty rode up after me and told me I was to go to the Shawanese towns.

"When we were come to the fire the Colonel was stripped naked, ordered to sit down by the fire and then they beat him with sticks and their fists. Presently after I was treated in the same manner. They then tied a rope to the foot of a post about fifteen feet high, bound the Colonel's hands behind his back and fastened the rope to the ligature between his wrists. The rope was long enough for him to sit down or walk around the post once or twice and return the same way. The Colonel then called to Girty and asked if they intended to burn him?—Girty answered, yes. The Colonel said he would take it patiently. Upon this, Captain Pipe, a Delaware chief, made a speech to the Indians consisting of about thirty or forty men and sixty or seventy squaws and boys.

"When this speech was finished, they all yelled a hideous and hearty assent to what had been said. The Indians then took up their guns, and shot powder into the Colonel's body from his feet up to his neck. I think not less than seventy loads were discharged upon him, and to my best observation, cut off his ears. When the crowd had dispersed a little, I saw blood trickling from both sides of his head in consequence thereof.

"Their fire was six or seven yards from the post to which the Colonel was tied, it was made of small hickory poles burnt quite through in the middle, each end of the poles remaining about six feet in length.

"Three or four Indians by turns would take up individually one of these burning pieces of wood, and apply it to his naked body already burnt black with powder. These tormentors presented themselves on every side of him so that in whichever way he ran round the post, they met him with burning fagots and poles. Some of the squaws took broad boards upon which they put a quantity of burning coals and hot embers, and threw on him; so that in a short time he had nothing to tread on but coals of fire and hot ashes to walk upon.

"In the midst of these extreme tortures, he called to Simon Girty and begged of him to shoot him; but Girty making no answer he called to him again. Girty then, by way of derision, told the Colonel he had no gun, at the same time turning about to an Indian who was behind him, laughed heartily, and by all his gestures seemed delighted at the horrid scene.

"Girty then came up to me and bade me prepare for death. He said, however, I was not to die at that place, but to be burnt at the Shawanese towns. He swore by G—d I need not hope to escape death, but should suffer it in all its extremities.

"He then observed, that some prisoners had given him to understand, that if our people had him they would not hurt him;

for his part, he said, he did not believe it, but desired to know my opinion of the matter, but being at that time in great anguish and distress for the torments the Colonel was suffering before my eyes, as well as the expectation of undergoing the same fate in two days, I made little or no answer. He expressed a great deal of ill-will for Col. Gibson, and said he was one of his greatest enemies, and more to the same purpose, to all of which I paid very little attention.

"Colonel Crawford, at this period of his suffering, besought the Almighty to have mercy on his soul, spoke very low, and bore his torments with the most manly fortitude. He continued in all the extremities of pain for an hour and three quarters or two hours longer, as near as I can judge, when at last, being almost exhausted, he lay down on his belly; then they scalped him, and repeatedly threw the scalp in my face, telling me, 'That was my great Captain.' An old squaw (whose very appearance in every way answered the ideas people entertain of the Devil) got a board, took a parcel of coals and ashes, and laid them on his back and head, after he had been scalped; he then raised himself upon his feet, and began to walk around the post; they next put a burning stick to him as usual, but he seemed more insensible of pain than before.

"The Indian fellow who had me in his charge now took me away to Capt. Pipe's house, about three quarters of a mile from the place of the Colonel's execution. I was bound all night, and thus prevented from seeing the last of the horrid spectacle. Next morning, being June 12th, the Indian untied me, painted me black, and we set off for the Shawanese town, which he told me was somewhat less than forty miles distant from that place. We soon came to the place where the Colonel had been burnt, as it was partly in our way; I saw his bones lying amongst the remains of the fire, almost burnt to ashes; I suppose after he was dead they laid his body on the fire. The Indian told me that was my big Captain, and gave the scalp halloo." *

---

* the scalp halloo—"A fearful yell; consisting of the sounds Aw and Oh, successively uttered, the last drawn out a great length—as long as the breath will hold, and raised about an octave higher than the first."

—Butterfield

Simon Girty to William Crawford at the Stake (from a poem by Frank Cowan)

You, naked as at birth, bound with a thong,
Will symbolize the Right enthralled by Wrong.

While I, in savage guise, will play my part,
The unseen Savage of the White Man's Heart.

Dr. John Knight

MILES NOW FROM PIPE'S TOWN where he was forced to watch the burning of Colonel Crawford who was taken during the retreat from Sandusky Plains. Crawford was taken at an unlucky time, coming when Girty's Wyandots were riled over the massacre of nearly 100 Christianized Delawares at Gnadenhutten. They had information that Crawford was marching under a black flag, a sign that he would spare no Indian regardless of age or sex. They knew that Crawford, true to the logic of the time, held the maxim, "nits breed lice." They also knew that Williamson, the commander of the expedition, had ordered the recent slaughter and had referred to it as a great victory. And that Crawford was his second in command. Given the choice, they would rather have had Williamson. But they didn't have him. They had Crawford, and Indian justice demanded that someone had to pay with his life. And Crawford burned.

So picture the two of them. The army surgeon Dr. Knight: middle-aged, smallish, his ears pointed and slightly lopsided like the halves of an elm leaf. Lapidary hands. A reedy man whose spectacles, a rare enough item then, gave him the near-sighted look of a scholar. They were the source of endless jokes among the Wyandots who had never seen anyone vain enough to wear ornaments on his nose rather than through it. You might say he was simply out of his element in the wilds. Badly shaken by what he had witnessed at Pipe's town, he was en route to a Shawnee town on Mad River where he was to be guest of honor at his own burning. To commemorate his doom, he was already painted black.

The second was his guard, a beanpole named Slow Knee who was chiefly distinguished by the penis-bone of a raccoon worn as a talisman dangling from his nose. This was an ornament other Wyandots could appreciate, even envy. Slow Knee on horseback, Dr. Knight on feet blistered taut as eggs, they covered 25 miles the first day, camping for the night on the edge of a bog. For safekeeping, Knight was bound to a sapling, the rawhide thong around his neck attached to Slow Knee's wrist. Neither got much sleep. The doctor spent most of the night trying to untie himself. Slow Knee spent most of it seeing that he didn't.

At daybreak they were beset by a peppery cloud of gnats, blood-sucking little devils that went for their heads, A swarm of them biting and humming that keen nasal hum in their ears. Knight asked that his hands be freed so he could shoo them. Slow Knee nodded okay and loosened the knots. Rubbing his wrists, Knight set about gathering deadfalls for a fire, the fire for its smoke. The idea was good, but they couldn't get one started. Though last night's ashes were still alive, the twigs, damp with morning, wouldn't catch. As Slow Knee knelt to blow the embers, Knight stole up behind and clobbered him on the head with a dogwood club. The dogwood broke, knocking Slow Knee headlong into the fire, his hands in the ashes. Though stunned and severely hurt, he was far from dead, or even unconscious. In fact, he was active, already moving, his instincts aiming him away from the hurt and toward shelter. Spying Slow Knee's rifle against a tree, Knight desperately grabbed it to finish him before he could get away, but was so excited he busted the mainspring trying to cock it. The gun was useless.

Terrified, Slow Knee scrambled to his feet and streaked off into the woods. His bellowing, Dr. Knight would recall, was shrill enough to turn leaves and drop them from the trees.

Gathering Slow Knee's powder, shot pouch, the broken rifle and flints, Knight considered his predicament. The horse was gone, having bolted when the commotion started. Lost, still painted black, nearly starved, he turned toward what he believed to be east and began his trek through the woods, where he wandered 21 days.

The first night he tried to get his bearings by the stars, but the sky was muddy with clouds. The second day he ate Slow Knee's last cornstick, and food became his major worry since water was plentiful, the woods being full of spring-fed branches. To make matters worse, his jaw was nearly broken by a tomahawk blow back at Pipe's town, and he could not chew. With these handicaps, he set out, knowing that no help was likely and that he must make it on what he could scavenge. The country he traveled was mostly swampland, low wet marshes filled with cranberry thickets (whose fruit had not yet ripened), Shaky ground, hard to keep a footing. He had the sensation that he was treading on an enormous sponge, and his feet turned sickly chalk. Several times he changed course to throw off the Indians he believed were dogging his trail. At one point he lost a day waiting for nightfall before crossing a prairie 16 miles wide. He was afraid the Indians would spot him and ride him down.

Crazy with fear, he saw Slow Knee in the trees and bushes, behind each rock, inside each sumac clump. He saw him in his sleep. Afraid to strike a fire, he was nearly devoured by woodgnats and mosquitoes. Oddly, he had no trouble finding game: deer, rabbits, even an elk, but had no way to kill them. One day he stumbled across a black bear with a young fawn in its jaws. When it spotted him, the bear, as scared as he was, dropped his kill and ran off. Knight, more terrified than hungry, hightailed it in the opposite direction.

By the tenth day he was light-headed, feverish, a little mad. But the jaws worked better, and he knew he must eat. Anything. He wore his finger ends to the quick picking soured hickory nuts. His diet during this time, each item noted carefully in his account, was roots, unripe gooseberries, young nettles, some May apples, two young blackbirds, and a terrapin. All eaten raw. A student of herbs, he took wild ginger to settle his stomach. On the 21st day, the 4th of July it so happened, he reached a great bluff from which he could survey the country. He looked out at an infinity of treetops, a stretch of unbroken lime whose edges blued on the horizon. Way off to the left, he spied a tiny thread of zinc-colored smoke rising above the treeline, the first human sign he had seen for three weeks. Fort McIntosh. Safety. A few hours later, in he hobbled, an eyesore, the rifle still clutched in one hand like a growth.

Speeches brought by Simon Girtie from the Six Nations to Detroit Feby 7th.

A Speech from the Women of the Six Nations Shawnese Delawars & Wyandots to the Warriours of all the different Nations.

Children: We wipe the Tears from your Eyes, and ease your Hearts for the loss of so many Young men We conjure you to forget our Misfortune. We gather their Bones together, and cover them lightly with leaves and a little Earth.

5 Strings of Wampum

Warriours: We the Old Men & Chiefs, join with the Women, in covering the Bodies of our deceased Friends with a few Branches.

Seven Strings of Wampum

Children: We have now eased your Hearts for the loss of our Friends, I now help you to stand firm and unloose the Strings I formerly tied your Feet with. To preserve you from all difficulties, we make your Mockasons of strong Buffaloe Leather, & Your

Leggins of Wolf-Skin, and we clothe you out in the best War dress. We have put new Strings to your Bows, and straighten'd your Arrors. That when you see your Enemies at a great distance you may be able to shoot thro' them.

15 Strings with a bit
of Tobacco

Girty Addresses the Grand Council of the Tribes at Chillecothe, Ohio, before Marching on Bryan's Station

"Brothers: the fertile region of Kentucky is the land of cane and clover—spontaneously growing to feed the buffaloes, the elk and the deer; there the bear and the beaver are always fat—the Indians from all the tribes have had a right from time immemorial to hunt and kill unmolested these wild animals and bring off their skins, to purchase themselves clothing—to buy blankets for their backs and rum to send down their throats, to drive away the cold and rejoice their hearts, after the fatigue of hunting and toil of war (great applause from the crowd). But

"Brothers: the long knives have overrun your country, and usurped your hunting grounds,—They have destroyed the cane—trodden down the clover—killed the deer and the buffaloes, the bear and the raccoon—They are building cabins and making roads on the ground of the Indian camp and warpath: The beaver has been chased from his dam and forced to leave the country (palpable emotion among the hearers).

"Brothers: the intruders on your lands exult in the success that has crowned their flagitious acts:—They are planting fruit trees and ploughing the land where not long since were the canebreak [*sic*] and clover field. Were there a voice in the trees of the forest, or articulate sound in the gurgling waters, every part of this country would call on you to chase away these ruthless invaders who are laying it waste:—Unless you rise in the majesty of your might and exterminate the whole race, you may bid adieu to the hunting ground of your whole race, you may bid adieu to the hunting ground of your fathers— to the delicious flesh of the animals with which it once abounded, and to the skins with which you were once enabled to purchase your clothing and your rum."

Girty the Provocateur

Visualize an egg in Girty's hand,
a turkey's,
perched frail among the knuckles.

Imagine this egg,
the thin shell, the pale embryo,
as all the white men west of Ft. Pitt,
the fist as Indians.

Now watch the fist,
the brittle membrane
as Girty squeezes,
clamping till the frailness pops
& hatches yellow pulp.

Judge the impression
on Black Hoof & Bad Bird
Blue Jacket, Little Turtle
Tarhe the Crane & White Loon
Shawnee & Wyandot
Miami Mohawk Mingo

Bryan's Station

THE FORT ITSELF CONTAINED about forty cabins, placed in parallel lines, connected by strong palisades, and garrisoned by forty or fifty men. It was a parallelogram of thirty rods in length by twenty in breadth (500 x 330 ft), forming an enclosure of nearly four acres, which was protected by digging a trench four or five feet deep, in which strong and heavy pickets were planted by ramming the earth well down against them. These were twelve feet out of the ground, being formed of hard, durable timber, at least a foot in diameter. Such a wall, it must be obvious, defied climbing or leaping, and indeed any means of attack, cannon excepted. At the angles were small squares or block-houses, which projected beyond the palisades and served to impart additional strength to the corners, as well as permitted the besieged to pour a raking fire across the advanced party of the assailants. Two folding gates were in front and rear, swinging on prodigious wooden hinges, sufficient for the passage in and out of men or wagons in times of security. These were of course provided with suitable bars.

—Henry Howe
*Historical Recollections
of The Great West*

Wm Calk's Journal

AUG YE 15TH 1782 SATTERDAY Bryans Station Awake this Day to fine the Fort surroundit by Indens Simon Girtee the renegaid & som Brittish, In plane sight the Savage 400 & more gathers Out Side whear they hide unter Brush and behine Stumps thier stratigem being to draw Our Fire that they may Lure us out to slawter. Each man to his gun we rais the Gates to Persue & they discharge thier peeces thierour Yells & screems frighting the womin & childern Indeed som Men but to no Effect a Few keeping Presents of Mine to clos the Gates. Capt. Craig sens 2 horse for Lexington we resolving to Holt until others com.

13 we choose amongst Our selfs to brave Out & trick the Indens others to lay by West wall whear we look for their attact. The Firing starts then Girtee him & his Indens rush to clime this Wall to his follie as the Men in waiting retirn Smart fire 20 or 30 is kiled in our Voleys,

at 2 oclock Capt. todd and his Men is ambusht on the Rode from Lexington the Indens lay all hid in a feeld of Corn. Those on horse com Safe But must fite thier way Those on foot scatters in Corn as the Inden yells &. shakes his Hatchits 6 being shot, yet One of ours shutes Girtee in the Brest who falls But is up agin as the Devil has put thick lether for Shoos In Side his Shert it doing no Harm, we luse 6 som Woondit 1 bad.

Sunday 16th: the Savage still with us. at 1 oclock Girtee struts him Out with flag of Truse & stans on a Stump thear to tel us that

surrender is serten as he expecks Canon Soon. He tels his Naim
bold & asks do we know it then Swares by his Honer no harm will
Com to Prisners but they Will be treet'd well. With much spearit
Young Reynolds Shouts back Indeed his naim is known unto him
As he Owns a worthies cur-Dog of that naim & that he may bring
Artillary & be d—D. Also if him & any Savage fine thier way In
Side they would chace them Out with swiches as we look for help
& should Girtee or any Savage remane 24 hours at the Fort thier
scalp will dry on the Roofs of cabins. Girtee Retreats in haste
when Reynolds asks Craig can he try a Shot. So the Indens shute
some agin To day with 4 kiled & 3 woondit but do Not Succeed in
Setting the walls afire. We shuting in all 30 or more enemy.

Aug. 17th Mond. the Seege is raysed No Inden being foun
only some Meets being Roast'd on sticks fires Smoking still the
Meets from our Catel.

Wounded at Bryan's Station

I feel the hate
grub its burrow in my skin
the lead globe
press my accessible heart.

Though it wallops me down
the flesh wont give,
the bullet blunt
against my second skin,
this leather.

As I fall in cornstalks,
my eye falls on
this one strung tassel,
one plump ear's hoard
of golden stones
my ripening will outlast.

Blue Licks

TWO DAYS LATER the last battle of the Revolution is fought. A disastrous defeat planned by Girty and made possible by a blunder of the Kentuckians. Within hours of Girty's pull-back from Bryan's Station, help from the outlying settlements begins to pour in. From Harrodstown comes a large force under Stephen Trigg. Daniel Boone brings thirty-odd rifles from Boonesborough, and John Todd rouses the militia at nearby Lexington. From farther away, Ben Logan is reported to be on route from St. Asaph's with a small army. By noon, 182 volunteers are armed and ready at the station, each man under his colonel, or colonels. The cream of Kentucky, they are eager, determined, a little cocky. Most of them have suffered from other raids, a heifer stolen or a barn burned. Many have lost a wife or a son, some a whole family. They are anxious to carry the fight back to its sources in die villages and towns north of the Ohio. Deal a blow there—destroy the corn crop, burn some huts—and the Indians would be hard put to strike again before winter.

A pow-wow is called and the leaders agree to cut the Indians off before they can cross the Ohio and make for their separate towns. Some mounted, some infantry, they hastily strike north, following a clearly marked trail. Too clearly marked. From the beginning the omens are bad. Instead of hiding their trail or moving roundabout, the Indians withdraw up a wide buffalo trace. No attempt is made to cover their tracks, as if they invite pursuit. If this isn't enough, trees are chopped down randomly along the trace as signs. White mounds of ashes are left in plain view. Camping that night in the woods, next day the volunteers reach the lower Blue Licks where they see their first Indians. Nearing the south bank of the Licking, they spy some stragglers scaling the rocky bluff across the river. They have crossed so recently, reddish silt they stirred still swims in the current. Almost casually, they pause at the summit, gazing down on the circus of men and horses, then leisurely pass out of sight.

Blue Licks is desolate country. Forsaken because it is the only wilderness for miles inhospitable to life. Situated in a craggy basin, it is the site of an ancient animal graveyard from the time when mammals came to lick salt and were preyed on by other mammals, hunters coming only later. The air is stale and salty like the inside of a meathouse and smells faintly of rancid flesh. Nothing blooms or prospers here. It is a place to be skirted or passed through quickly. The ground is very rough, cluttered with large moss-covered boulders, which follow the trace as it rises out of the river bottom onto the steep ridge. Even trees are sparse, the terrain being too rocky. Only scrub and a few cedars poke out of the slopes, rock-loving trees that thrive on meager soil. Thousands of buffalo, uncountable generations, have stamped out all vegetation along the trail. The earth is scooped out in a kind of trough, hard and smooth as clay, engineered with animal efficiency along the easiest grade.

At the ford, a second pow-wow is called to devise a strategy for attack. The old heads have their say first. Todd the aristocrat sagely asks the opinion of Boone who is well acquainted with the Licks, having been captured almost on the spot by the Shawnee Blackfish a few winters back while boiling salt for Boonesborough. His visit had been prolonged because 600 gallons of the brackish water were needed to produce one bushel of salt, Boone, whose body except for a small rabbit paunch is a study in thrift and serviceable vigor, has survived Indians longer than any of them. Cool-headed and uncannily acute, he describes the situation as "tetchy." Extremely delicate, Todd agrees. The Indians outnumber them. The obvious trail and sluggish retreat are suspicious. The more so since the spot is ideal for an ambush. Given these facts, Boone counsels they wait for Logan to join them and then to proceed only with great caution. If they are to attack now, he advises they split in two parties and march against the Indians' rear. In any case, he recommends a thorough scout of the area before doing anything. His words make an impression. Everyone, even the hotheads, goes thoughtful for one long moment. You can hear the tobacco churning in a hundred jaws, the creaking of leather as weight is shifted in the saddles. Nearly two hundred men in deep river shade, some asquat on white stones, others hunkered against sycamores, a few already whittling as they blink in sun-glare which banks off the water and shimmers in the leaves. No one really believes a band of marauding savages will stand to such a force. They just won't. They never have before.

The pause is broken by Hugh McGary, a blustery Irishman. Without waiting for a decision, he raises a war whoop and spurs his horse into the river, waving his hat around his frugal Irish head. Halfway across, he turns and shouts a dare for all who aren't craven cowards to follow him. And they do. The effect is magnetic. Every man-jack, horse and foot alike, plunges into the green water, half-swimming, half-wading across the neck high ford. They blunder across in a miscellaneous mass of animals and men, McGary, followed by Majors Harlan and McBride, is still in the lead.

Across the river now, regaining its momentum, the mass streams helter-skelter up the ridge. No scouts are sent ahead. No one is sent to examine the flanks. The ground levels somewhat along the sharp spines of the ridge, aptly called a hogback. The buffalo trail, still keeping the path of least resistance, follows the ridge-line, two deep ravines gaping on either side of it, both filled with dense thickets of honeysuckle and Virginia creeper. The hermit thrushes whose twitters ordinarily fill the woods are not missed as the momentum gathers again, those in the rear getting their wind back as they reach level ground.

This is their pattern as they assemble on the ridge. Boone is on the left. Trigg is on the right. The mounted force, led by Todd, Harlan, McGary, and McBride, hold to the center. This is their pattern when the horsemen, nearly a half-mile from the river, run headlong into a party of Indians. Most of the leaders are killed in the first volley. Those in the rear, hearing the gunfire and rushing up to assist, find themselves caught in a deadly crossfire from the ravines on either side of them. Taking what cover they can, they return fire but with less effect since the Indians are well concealed and they are caught on naked ground.

In seconds the whole ridge is mantled in blue smoke, so thick tlic eyes of the combatants run with powder burns. Everyone loses his bearings. Those not killed in the first exchange fire aimlessly into the maze of thickets which face the ravines. If seeing is difficult, hearing is not. The rifle reports, the baying of the horses, the squawls of the injured are deafening.

As the fighting grows more intense, Girty gradually extends the Indian line, forming a horseshoe around the Kentuckians to cut off their retreat. Discovering this maneuver, the surviving riders, most of their leaders dead, break for the river, each man for himself. Pressed sharply, the rear now falters and joins the run for the water, the open end of the horseshoe. In moments the retreat becomes a rout, the rout a slaughter as the Wyandots shout the scalp halloo, drop their rifles, and join the race. Many retreating are overtaken at the river bank or shot in the water. Some even drown. A private named Netherland, reaching the far bank ahead of the others, dismounts and calls on those around him to reform and fire on the Indians. Surprisingly, many do, and the Wyandots are held back long enough to give those in the water sufficient time to cross and make good their escape.

Once on the other side, the rout loses its center and shears off in all directions on the open ground. Most of the mounted men stick to the road. Those on foot, afraid of being overtaken there, rush blindly into the woods. In minutes the fighting is finished. Failing to press their advantage, many of Girty's Wyandots stop to take scalps and squabble over the spoils—the choicest rifles, the likeliest mounts.

As it is, the defeat is devastating. The Licking is awash with blood, pink clots which form smoky circlets, dissolve, and are whisked off by the current. Todd, Harlan, Trigg, McBride, and the Bulger brothers are among the dead, as are most of the officers. Boone's son Israel is one of the first to fall, drilled by a bullet through the neck. Boone himself is nearly killed trying to drag the body away from the fighting. Sixty-six men in all are lost. Four are captured. Two will be ransomed, two burned. McGary survives. As for Girty's force, they suffer minor losses. Ten dead plus a Frenchman named Le Bute.

Benjamin Logan, arriving two days later to bury the corpses, has no trouble locating them. Scores of glutted turkey buzzards drift in tipsy circles over the battlefield. What's left of the bodies is bloated and butchered beyond recognition. Those in the river have been gnawed on by fish. The remains are pieced and gathered, then buried in a mass grave. Stupified, overcome with the loss of so many close friends, Logan can find no words to say over the gravesite. Not one Indian was found on the battlefield. As is customary, the Indians have collected their dead and carried them away.

Girty, the victor, has staged his greatest coup. He is jubilant. Everywhere he will be esteemed and made over. Never has his influence over his following been greater. Out-maneuvered, out-fought by a zealous and calculating party of Wyandots, Shawnees, Delawares, and a sprinkling of Ottawas, Chippewas, and Mohawks, the Kentuckians are whipped in a battle that lasts no more than five minutes.

The Knob

I AM STANDING ON THE KNOB. The cedar a few feet away has been shagged by a bullet, strands of stringy red fiber splintered from the perfect cylinder of its trunk. From here to the river is a carpet of corpses, some red, some white, but this time mostly white. From this distance, though, there is little difference. Men painted in garish colors are stooping along the carpet, busy stripping and picking, stroking hair from the smoking scalps. Some are crowing for joy. Others are cutting capers, cutting heads.

The afternoon is turning bleak. The surface of the water is black, dunked in shadow, depthless. Near the bank several bodies are caught in the roots of a sycamore, played by the currents. The woods beyond are somber, vague now, no limb distinct from any other in the mesh of trees. Most of them are stripped and leafless, but the oaks are just turning, crimson swatches against the hazy thatching. Every once in a while, a rifle shot, stretched and swaddled with distance, breaks over the sky and sinks trembly in the bottoms. Stragglers. The light goes slack along the bluff. Soon it will rain autumn rain.

Chambers' Mill, Granville, Kittanning, Cattaraugus, Ft. Pitt, Detroit, Chillicothe, Bryan's Station; a hundred named and nameless places in the woods. And now Blue Licks, atop this saltbed between the races, looking down on spoiling meat, white meat, what minutes ago were men hankering for my scalp, the bounty on my head. Now they lie gaping and wasted along this slope, so many broken crocks, their swagger and hate stiffening in this chill air their blood won't know. Faces I have known from far points and some I've known close from Pitt or Dunmore days. Masks now, eyes locked on pain, their expressions open to read, placid, surprised, stupid with fear. Stone. These won't come closer. Today, their uncles and brothers claim that side of the river. Soon, a few days, a few years, they will cross to this one. Then this will happen again and maybe that time they will win. But now, here, lone in the cedars, my time is come. This moment is my feast. It was all so easy. . . .

ESCAPE

A Progress Report

IN JULY OF 1770 CASPER MANSKER and his party of Long Hunters, returning from the wilds, heard a strange sound far off in the woods. A kind of bellowing, neither animal nor even remotely human. Investigating, they came to a small meadow where they found Daniel Boone stretched out naked on a deerskin, singing nonsense at the top of his lungs. Boone, who had spent months wandering solitary through the Red River country without seeing one human sign, had dropped all precaution, believing himself to be alone.

Population of Kentucky

in 1790:	61,133 whites
	12,430 slaves
	114 free blacks
	73,677 total
in 1800:	220,959 total souls

The bees had found the honey.

The influx of settlers into the Kentucky country by flatboat, keelboat, raft, pirogue, by wagon, horse, and foot, was by two routes. Georgians, Carolinians, Virginians, and others from the southern regions entered from Powell's Valley in southwestern

Virginia through a gap in the Alleghenies at Cumberland Mountain (named by Dr. Thomas Walker, the first recorded white man to pass through it, for the Duke of Cumberland). Once through the mountains, they traveled west for fifty or so miles along the ancient Warrior's Path, the Athiamio-wee, then followed a buffalo trace west to Hazel Patch in Rockcastle County. There the road forked, the northern route going on to Boonesboro and the Bluegrass, the western branch to Crab Orchard and St. Asaph's, then on to Danville, Bardstown, and Jefferson County to the Falls of the Ohio, where Louisville, a natural stopping place, was taking shape as a city.

The second more popular but more hazardous route was by water from Redstone on the Monongahela and Ft. Pitt in western Pennsylvania down the Ohio River to Limestone (the town Kenton named, later called Maysville) and overland to the Bluegrass on the Limestone-Lexington Trace [the buffalo trail that Todd and his volunteers followed to disaster at Blue Licks in '82]. Some traveled farther down the Ohio and up the Kentucky River [the Louisa, Luvisa, Cuttawa, Cuttaw-ba], the Indian highway which cut a deep gorge through the Inner Bluegrass.

Who came: tinkers, river rats, millwrights, drovers, runaways, disinherited second sons, lawyers, scoundrels, scoundrel lawyers, ring-tailed roarers, speculators, land-grabbers, slaves, snake doctors, innkeepers, bluebloods, Yankee peddlers, Swiss and German farmers, Ulster-Irish, blacksmiths, silversmiths, gunsmiths, cobblers, felons, backwoods trappers, emigrés, teamsters, horsebreeders, dandies, wheelwrights, Virginians (Jefferson crossed the mountains only in name), ferrymen, vagabonds, yeomen, army deserters, land-granted veterans, preachers, mechanics, pork-barrel demagogues, a black fiddler named Cato, a bishop in the Methodist Church, a painter of birds.

The estimated cost: Judge Harry Innes, Attorney General of the District of Kentucky, estimated that between the close of the Revolutionary War and 1790, a period of seven years, the Indians had slain 1,500 settlers and stolen 20,000 horses, besides destroying immense quantities of other property, real and personal. Not to mention the territories bordering Kentucky.

One of the first recorded casualties was Boone's hunting companion John Stuart, who crossed to the south side of the Kentucky to hunt and explore on his own, promising to return in two weeks. He was never seen again. Missing him at their rendezvous, Boone found Stuart's trail, a recent fire, even his initials carved in a tree. But no Stuart.

Five years later when Boone was blazing a trail for the Wilderness Road, one of his men found a skeleton in a hollow sycamore near the Rockcastle River. The left arm had been shattered at the elbow by a bullet. There was no sign of a rifle, but the powder horn found with the bones had a brass band with the initials J.S.

Aborigines in 1800: No census, but diminished, diminishing.

Even when threatened, most wild animals do not move in straight courses. Take the rabbit in winter. The snow serves as a kind of ledger recording his motions. His tracks, little stabbings in the crust, some messy, some clean, proceed in a direct line for a few hops, then veer. Invariably, he will sidestep to sniff a scent or circle a stump, sometimes pausing on his hind legs, his grooved ears turning in the air like antennae. Probing and withdrawing, he changes direction constantly. He makes diversions and feints. He does this for survival. Occasionally, his urine will poke yellow cylinders in the snow. His crooked path is punctuated with tiny mounds of dark pellets whose perfectly formed pyramids resemble stacked cannonballs. Such was the course of the Northwestern tribes during the Indian wars until about 1800 when either the snow melted or the tracks just disappeared.

The following are where some of the pellets piled. In 1774 Lord Dunmore's War was precipitated by a scoundrel named Daniel Greathouse, who for the sport of it tortured and murdered the family of Logan, a theretofore peaceful chief of the Delawares. Greathouse lured the Indians to his camp, got them drunk, and systematically shot them, down to the last child. The unborn papoose of Logan's sister was cut from her belly and stuck up on a pole. Logan vowed to take ten lives for each member of his family and bettered himself before sending his famous speech to Lord Dunmore:

"Who is there to mourn for Logan? Not one." Girty, still a scout for Dunmore's army, delivered and translated the speech into English.

The highlight of the campaign was the Battle of Point Pleasant, considered by many to be the first battle of the Revolution, a disaster in which the Virginians under Gen. Andrew Lewis lost half of their commissioned officers and fifty-two militiamen, seventy-five men in all. The Indians under Cornstalk lost twenty-two killed and eighteen wounded. Some early histories had it erroneously that Girty defected to the Indians before the battle and directed them during the attack.

During 1777, "The Year of the Bloody Sevens," all three of Kentucky's original settlements were attacked: Boonesboro, Ft. Harrod, Logan's Station, When Boonesboro came under siege again two years later, the defenders afterwards recovered 125 pounds of lead from the fort's walls.

In May of 1779 Col. John Bowman carried the war to the Indians' homeland in Ohio, With 262 men he attacked Chillicothe, the town where Kenton stole his horses, and set fire to it. Though most of the inhabitants were elsewhere, a few old men led by Chief Black Fish put up a defense in the council house and managed to stave off the attack. Despite Bowman's ineptness, the expedition was deemed a success, netting 163 Indian ponies and other plunder, including silver ornaments and clothing amounting in all to $160,000 Continental money. For payment each man received $500 in goods or horses. The biggest loss to the Shawnees was Black Fish, their principal chief.

The following year Col. Henry Byrd with six field pieces and 1,600 Canadians and Indians compelled the surrender of Ruddell's and Martin's stations in northern Kentucky. Unable to stop his Indians from massacring the prisoners, he retreated north across the river rather than proceed. Appalled and perhaps a little finicky, he called off what could have been a clean sweep of Kentucky. Girty, who was along with his Wyandots, was disappointed.

To retaliate, Gen. George Rogers Clark at the head of 1,000 men destroyed the Piqua (Pick-a-way) towns on the Miami, including over 800 acres of corn. A sub-tribe of the Shawnees, the Piquas believed in a mythological progenitor, "a man of majestic form and godlike mien," who burst out of a sacred fire on the site during a religious convocation of the entire Shawnee Nation. "Piqua" means "a man risen from the ashes," Piqua did not, as the Phoenix, rise out of its ashes. The magic did not work a second time.

Six years later Gen. Clark led another expedition, this time against the Wabash Indians at Mackachack in Indiana. There, Moluntha, the Shawnee King, was murdered after he surrendered. Clark succeeded in destroying thirteen towns: Mackachack, Moluntha's Town, Mingo Town, Wapatomica, Mamacomink, Kispoco, Pucksha-noses, McKee's Town, Waccachalla, Chillicothe, Peco-wick, Buchangehelas' Town, and Blue Jacket's Town.

Not all the campaigns were bloodbaths. In 1787 Col. Bowman led another expedition to the Ohio country. This time his target was the Great Miami River towns. He met no resistance. The only Indians he could discover were some squaws picking blackberries in a field. Afterwards, his expedition was called "The Blackberry Campaign."

Four years later the young republic suffered the worst military disaster (up to that time) in its history; "St. Clair's Defeat." Six hundred thirty-two of the 930 men engaged were killed, among them Gen. Richard Butler, second in command of the entire American army. The battle took place 23 miles north of Greenville, Ohio, in Darke County. Indians under Blue Jacket, Buchange-helas, and Girty chased St. Clair's routed campaigners 29 miles back to Ft. Jefferson. Added to the casualties were 56 camp followers. The battle was the last in which Girty played an active part.

After St. Clair's Defeat, Girty was said to have set up a trading-house, first at Lower Sandusky and then on the St. Mary's River at a spot which came to be known as Girty's Town, the present site of St. Mary's in Mercer County, Ohio. When "Mad Anthony" Wayne passed through that country in 1794 on his way to "Fallen Timbers," Girty got word. Afraid of what would be done to him if he were captured, he abandoned his goods and took to the hills.

The battle that followed marked the last major resistance of the Northwestern Indians in the Ohio country, Theodore Roosevelt in his *Winning of the West* described it as the end of an era. On the heels of his victory, Wayne destroyed the villages along the Auglaize and Maumee Rivers, including Alexander McKee's trading post. McKee himself, accompanied by his sidekicks Matt Elliott and Girty, witnessed the fighting from a very respectable distance.

These, then, were some of the recorded spots where pellets were stacked in the snow. More numerous were the thousands of nameless encounters, bushwhackings, and skirmishes in the woods, incidents where the tracks began and then just disappeared. As, for example, Boone's account of coming upon a solitary Indian fishing from a fallen tree over a stream somewhere in the wilds of Kentucky. "As I was looking at the fellow," Boone joked, "he tumbled into the water, and I saw him no more."

Girty's Vision
of the Future

I see the corn in puckered rows
the stumps of squandered trees
the landscape tamed with fences
ruts cut by metal wheels.

I see the skulls of buffalo
bone commas stacked in piles
plucked turkey wings & Indian hair
words twisting black as rivers.

The land made fit for Christians
stiff trophies on each wall
the hobby of extinction
made universal law.

Convergence

To feel the instant when Tecumseh,
"The-Panther-Star-Passing-Across,"
hears his first iron-hooped wheel
grate against the creekbed.

He hesitates. He listens
as the newness
builds its image in his mind.

Midstroke, he holds
his scalloped flint scraper
above the elkhide
that will last 10 winters.

Mad River

WHAT STOPS MY EYE ARE THE LEGS, especially the calves. Not the shape, mind you, so much as the color. White as hominy. That pasty pearl you find on mussel shells in parched streambeds, the slightest marbling in the cup where thin light spills. Almost iridescent. Not really a wilderness color. Not what you'd expect here unless you are familiar with the undersides of fawns and rabbits, the plumage of some marsh birds, or bones. Unusual because it does not belong here, does not belong because it's free of the blush or blemish things take on as they live and rub against other things, wear down. Background is what makes it show, for a plum will stand out in broth. The more surprise to discover this white in the scruff and dinge of a Delaware camp.

She is sitting cross-legged in a circle of squaws, six or eight of them gossiping around a fire, one or two tending earth-colored babies, the rest shelling corn, I watch the rough, competent hands as they husk each ear, scraping the yellow kernels onto a slab of scooped-out stone which serves as a mortar. One grinds the kernels into meal with a crude sandstone pestle the size of a man's fist, bits of flaky gold seeping out from the edges into a bowl. When I stare too long, they stop their gabbling and turn their eyes to the work. Except for hers, which lift to mine, curious, a trifle surprised.

The face does not give her away. The skin is buffed suede, a shade paler than copper, smoke-smudged in places, the features framed by a wreath of brown hair wantonly tangled. Nor the clothes. Tanned mocassins she herself has likely chewed the softness into. A leathern petticoat. Skin greased with bearfat to ward off insect stings and chiggers. Far from feminine, her only adornment is a necklace, a polished cylinder of some dark stone, maybe obsidian, hanging from a thong between the hummocks of her breasts—which my eyes keep coming to. Her total appearance is more Indian than white, yet she retains something residually soft, pliant. Not dainty or extravagant, but with some inborn gift that sets her off from the others, that claims the life she lives is not the one she was born to. She is like a porcelain chip fired into some earthenware, a coin embedded in the reddish grit, but smoother, more lustrous. What the loafers at Ft. Pitt would call a prime article.

By nightfall I have her history. Her name is Catherine Malott and she is nineteen, almost exactly half my age. Four years before, her family was heading down the Ohio from Maryland to the Kentucky settlements. Near Wheeling at Captina Creek they were set upon by a band of Delawares under Washnash, their flatboat having run aground on a sandbar. The entire family, brothers, sisters, mother, was taken except for the father who managed somehow to escape across the river. Not long after, they separated her from her kin, for breaking ties made entry into the tribe much easier. She was adopted by a family of Munceys, an offshoot clan of the Delawares. Her foster family had lost their only daughter to smallpox. For four years she lived with them on Mad River, surviving partly because she was young, partly because her new parents went soft on her. Though she was no longer watched, escape was impossible, unthinkable for a girl, alone, without food or the means to get any. The nearest white settlement, Dunlap's, was over two-hundred miles east. So she made the most of her captivity. And bided. The Munceys call her O-wa-ta-wa. White Pigeon.

Next morning I am back. Still no words have passed between us. Her eyes, deep-set and almost guileless, bind me to her, feed my curiosity.

The third morning there is a change. Her hair is free of straggles, bound neatly behind her neck. The eyes are more trusting. And more—this third time she talks, or tries to. She has not spoken English for four years, almost one fifth of her life, and must tame her tongue to form the sounds, school her wits to fashion phrases and sentences again. The words come out foreign at first, thick with Delaware gristle, sounds which start deep in the throat and flick off the tongue. But gradually she improves. Gradually the rust leaves her speech and she shapes her words close and natural. Clear enough to beg I take her with me to Detroit.

Catherine Malott

WHAT I SAW across the fire that day was not the ugly cut on his forehead or the intentions behind his look. Not even his age: the creases by his mouth, the bunching in his shoulders. These sights and more came later. What I saw or didn't see, was the chin. In its place was a tangle of black wires joining to become a beard. Three years since I had seen hair on a chin, a white chin dirty as it was. Three years. This beard was not kempt but hung in greasy strings and climbed his cheeks until it mingled with the sideburns and the mass of matted hair. The face, neither handsome nor unpleasant, was always tensed, surrounded by bristly hair, the skin inside heart-shaped like an owl's.

To the others he was no prize, no one to make over. Traders before the war had frequently stopped here on their way to Detroit or south to the Ohio, though fewer since. But for me, the beard was a ladder, a road to the settlements. White settlements and family. For me it meant deliverance, escape. Or the hope of it.

Simon Girty The Outlaw: An Historical Romance by Uriah Jones

WILD WITH PASSION, glowing with excitement, and flushed with success, Edith soon fell a victim to his snares. She was stung with remorse, and shuddered as she thought of him who had led her to the altar, and swore to love and protect her, when he made her his own. What a painful contrast with him she loved, who by artifice had forced her from her husband's arms, and now held her, as what?—his mistress! She knew it, and keenly she felt her degradation. . . . Time wore away, and the spirit of Edith was crushed, but her kind heart won for her many friends among the Indians, and there was not one among the whole tribe, either man, woman or child, who did not love and esteem her; yet misery, that foul cankerworm, was eating its way silently through her heart.

Time wore away, and the Outlaw's love for Edith became lukewarm. He no more greeted her with the burning kiss, or sat for hours pouring in her ears those welcome tales of love that first won her heart twelve years ago.

Time wore away, the Outlaw's passion was gratified, and he no longer cared for Edith, but met her with a look of cool indifference.

Time wore away, and the Outlaw treated Edith with the same contempt that brutal, selfish man ever metes out to the woman over whose virtue he had triumphed, and whose charms have faded.

Time wore away, and the Outlaw commenced wooing of the Indian maidens. The gentle confiding Edith was deserted by the man who had torn her from her husband's arms, and despised by him for being what he himself had made her.

The beautiful Nuschetto was as lovely an Indian maiden of fifteen, as ever graced a Delaware town, and many a warrior sighed in vain for her hand. . . .

Girty's Town

JUST ME AND LEATHERLIPS. Awright you win, I say, offering to swap him 5 jugs and some vermilion for the lot. Which is 6 prime deerskin, 55 otter, 10 beaver, 2 bear, and a dozen or so young mink. Mah-tah, matah, he says, not enough. Rapping the heel of his right hand in the saddle of his left, driving the syllables in hard, the shells around his neck tinkling like nervous bells.

This give and take goes on an hour or so, neither of us budging. No trade. He won't give in for pride and ordinary cussedness. I won't on principle, knowing that if I do every Wyandot and Shawnee this side of Ft. Pitt will sense my weakness and hike the prices higher. And this I can't let happen. Better to loaf at Girty's Town and chew sour pork than dicker over a few hides. All this squaw talk.

Leatherlips does not see it this way. When he makes one last bid and I refuse, he turns surly. Goading, he asks why did I lift the siege at Bryan's Station, his gist being I did it because I was scared I might fall into hands of the militia we knew was coming. Hot now myself, I am on my feet heading for the cool, dry corner where the powder's stored. I choose a smaller keg—still quite enough to add a cellar to my hut—and fetch it to the fire, his sass wilting into outright fear as I snatch a brand from the ashes and place it still smoking an inch or so from the lid, the glowing stick between us like a fuse. This long enough for him to know I mean it. And Leatherlips, pouting a little even as the fear prods him toward the doorway, knowing he will lose face, his hides stacked neat and decent on the floor. The last thing I see is his greasy breechclout as he ducks into daylight.

Haven

IT IS BITTER COLD and the woods are still. The trees are frozen to their roots, gray trunks rigid in their brittle bark. The Month of the Hard Moon. My breath, warm as it leaves my mouth, forms little mushroom clumps that melt as they meet the cold, bloom for an instant, then melt again. Though the mulch is deep here, the woods strewn with leaf-fall, the cold has squeezed out its moisture until the game path beneath my feet is hard and trackless as stone. And cold, the weather gradually working up through the fur lining of my moccasins and settling in the balls of my knees, the pit of my groin, chiseling at my joints. The old pain resident in my feet again. Chilblains. An aching rheumatic damp no fire can quicken, which comes from too much water in the limbs, too many winters padding on animal skins. A stone cold deep in the bones that won't be cured. It is not the cold of winter which kills. It is the sameness. As though the world and everything in it has made a pact, each leaf locked in its sliver of ice, the ground drawn in on itself and niggard, a hatchet face of glazed blue steel, its surface the texture of a frozen blanket, a nap of rasping frost, all softness kinked out of it.

Since crossing the ice-sheet over the Scioto this morning, I have the feeling I am not alone. Not that I have seen anything unusual, not that the undercurrent of forest sounds my ear knows has changed in any way. Nothing so certain. Yet I sense a presence, something deeper though less substantial than signs—a scattering of birds or a string of coral-berries snapped from their bush. It is more a stirring in the blood, a whiff of something foreign known only by the animal in me. Bounty-hunters there have been and will be. It is no secret Congress and Pennsylvania have placed a price of 500 guineas on my head, prize enough to tempt red friends as well as foes.

My first impulse is to discount these messages as fancy, as fatigue or even jitters. Yet a quarter hour later a mile away, the feeling comes again. The presence not ahead of me, but somewhere behind. Re-priming my piece with dry powder and checking the flint, I trot a few hundred yards farther along the trail, then veer abruptly uphill past a cropping of rocks and onto a wooded plateau. There I stop, picking for cover a large scabby oak where I can watch the trail without being seen.

All day I keep my lockout, not daring to kindle a fire, scarcely taking my eyes from the trail. My feet and hands go so numb I am afraid of frostbite again. I dwell on images of fire, logs flaking into coals, cooking stones with their store of warmth, smoke smells. Toward mid-afternoon I sense the presence again, but it takes the form of a cautious rabbit grubbing buds in a patch of sassafras beside the trail. Another time toward dusk the black shape of a curious hawk rakes its shadow across the ridge, gliding once or twice over my lockout, the fingers in its wings tipping slightly before dropping into the cast of stricken trees. Though I comb the path, there is no trace of the rabbit.

Too late to take the trail again, I must search shelter for the night. There are plenty of overhangs among the boulders, dry crevices with their small bones and dust, but they are too exposed. Then farther up the slope I spot a giant beech with the top blown out of it, probably struck by lightning, possibly by a tornado or wind storm. Approaching, I see that it is long dead. The seamless gray bark girding its heart is split by scrawls.

Black wrinkles spread across its surface like writing. Crow's feet. Here and there are stubby branchlets, perpendicular and wobbly out of proportion with the monstrous trunk, a few skimpy orange leaves still clinging to their tips. Several dark sockets in the upper trunk tell me that it is hollow. Sure enough, when I reach its backside, there is a fork-shaped opening at the roots, three, maybe three and a half feet high. To each side of it the bark is folded neatly like furled cloth. Stooping, I peer into the darkness and see knots of yellow light in the upper trunk. After removing my shot pouch and chewing my last few mouthfuls of jerked meat, I release the hammer on my rifle and place it barrel-up inside the tree. Crouching, headfirst I snake my way through and into its center. Though the entry is close, inside I find room enough to stand and some to spare. The walls are rough and pulpy, bored through with thousands of tiny holes. More earth than wood, the punk scales off easily and I am able to shape footholds at either side and so raise my feet out of the opening.

Gradually, gouging out stirrups as I go and using my elbows as levers, I work my way upwards until I can just put my eye to a peephole and survey the slope below. Which is clear. Wedged as I am between these great soft slabs of rotting wood, protected from the weather, I am surprisingly comfortable. Though I cannot stretch out, I am fixed snugly within the tunnel, my feet no longer cold. The cloying smell of dry-rot fills my nostrils, the deep rich scent of decomposing wood. That night, sheathed in my rotting beech, I learn to sleep standing. I dream of fungus in papery hooves, rabbits in their burrows, squirrels, red-furred and dreamless, in their nests.

Tracker

He takes me from behind,
the muscles harnessed tight
around my neck
before I see him

the tourniquet he twists
so taut, the wind halts
in my lungs

the small black pennies
clogging in my veins,
their lazy pockets stagnant
till the sugar flows

and my elbow finds
the fencing of his ribs,
my thumbs the plump dove
nesting in his throat

till I must stand here
gawking at my hands,
bloodless now and dreaming spoons,
this single blister,
a white cloud drifting on my palm.

The Trail

I WAKE, my legs live with stinging, my heels sunk in spongy dirt of the mound. An anthill. All night I have slept on a colony of ants. This spot I chose to drop my robes last night. I feel them over my body now. On the plateau of my chest, the ridges and valleys of my arms and legs, my back. Their bites ignite little pricks of pain along my skin, not deep or lasting but irksome. The hair-scratchy feel of them as they scale my forearm, red raw-looking welts where they bit me in my sleep. Red ants. Whole constellations on me, each a cluster of shiny red beads, six legs twisted fine and nervous, feelers like spare feet sticking out of the forehead. Scuffing them off my arms, slapping them in my leggins. Scraping. A tingly feel and itchiness around the ankles, me mashing the beads which stick in the black prairies of my shins. Nothing large enough to loose my rage on, dirt things on me acting brash.

Onto my feet now, still groggy. The mound is three feet across and over half as high. Fine grains of dirt piled up, a few tufts of grass poking from the summit. The surface pitted with small tunnels like pores. The mouth of each is crowded with guards. Ants scurrying every which way, crisscross, in and out like needles through cloth, the hill shivering with motion as I direct my stream onto it, a yellow arc wetting and crumbling the passageways, pittering in dark blotches which join solid dark, then puddling and soaking through, drowning some.

But this is not enough. Jabbing and sweeping the busy maze of passages now with the butt of my musket, its curved brass heel

159

churning the maze into ruts, crazy furrows. Mussing what's left with my heel, tamping the looseness hard and final. My own small erosion, my own small avalanche. And this still not enough.

FIVE DOLLARS REWARD

BROKE AWAY OR WAS STOLEN FROM THE RAILING OF PETER JANUARY'S AT LIMESTONE ON THE NIGHT OF THE 26TH INST

A SORREL MARE

ABOUT 14 HANDS HIGH, WELL MADE, BLAZED FACE AND RATHER FLAT, ABOUT 4 OR 5 YEARS OLD, TROTS AND CANTERS WELL, SHOD ALL ROUND, SHORT TAIL WHICH SHE CARRIES WELL, IS REMARKABLY SPIRITED, NO BRAND RECOLLECTED, WITH A NEW HANDSOME, DOUBLE SKIRTED SADDLE, BLUE CLOTH WITH TWO ROLLS OF RED TRIMMING LEATHER SURSINGLE, BRIDLE TOLERABLY NEW REINED WITH BLACK LEATHER AND MORROCO BROWBAND, PLATED STIRRUP IRONS ALSO PLATED CURB

RETURN TO

MR. ROBERT BRADLEY, OR CAPT. JOHN POSTELWAIT OF THIS PLACE OR TO HUBBARD TAYLOR OF BOURBON COUNTY AND REASONABLE CHARGES PAID

Kentucky Gazette Apr 20th 1788

Cottonwood

BOUND FOR MALDEN after some weeks hunting to the south, I camp one night at a spring on the edge of a vast grassland. It is dusk. The tree shadows, sprawled and dozing around my feet, are the last for miles, at least as far as I can see. Beyond them is a span of rolling hills, subtle humps and rises covered with deep-rooted grasses, limber tongues. Tall shafts of cane, still winter-sallow, rise out of the humps in random patches, some probably a mile across. Behind me is the thick knit of shadow, three hundred miles of wilderness. The space between these two is neutral. Its air is neither prairie nor woodland but hybrid, smelling of damp leaves and animal oils, yet sparser, the scents combed thin by grasses and rinsed of all sound but the chirruping of two meadowlarks, one a few feet away.

I feel them before I hear them, hear them before I see them. Buffalo. Hundreds, maybe thousands of buffalo spilling over the rim of hills, thick as black bees when the locusts flower. I am filling my canteen at the spring when it happens. Ground under me begins to quake and tremble. I feel thunder in my ribs, a thumping as if my body were the stretched skin on a drumhead. Then the springwater begins to shimmy, just quivers in its pool, blurring the bottom out of focus. I hear something like the rush of wind through leaves before a cloudburst, a rumbling, troubled sound, but louder, tenser, charged with authority. It can't be weather, for the sky is blank, cloudless.

Then off to the east I spot a puff of white dust on the horizon. It blossoms toward me, the low roar growing with the bloom which yellows as it nears. I can make out details now, the curly heads packed close to form an unbroken wall of hooves and humps, horns lowered and glossed among the black bodies, thick winter coats not shed yet. The size of them. Some bulls must be over 6 feet from hoof to hump, some the length of two ponies.

I am in the tree now, a cottonwood, 20 feet above them. I cannot see the ground for buffalo, for tons of hides and huffing steaks. Though it looks like they will pass 50 rods or so from my tree, at the last minute they turn suddenly and head straight for my lookout. They are close enough for me to see the flakes of dirt flung off the leaders' hooves, black clods and pelts of stringy turf, lolling pink tongues. No grunts or whines come from them. Rather, the only sound is their weighted hooves, so many falling stones, and these crowd my ears to popping. Each is intent on motion, on keeping his place in the herd. A few feet away, the leaders swerve slightly, weave round my tree, and join again, still running, never once breaking stride. This is done routinely with that strange grace shared by bulky things and dancers.

Now I think of my horse, the stray I haltered a few weeks ago outside one of the river settlements, a sorrel mare socked white to her shanks. But too late. Before drinking at the spring, I tethered her to a sapling a dozen or so yards away. She is absolutely frantic. Her eyes are bugged out of her head and she is bleeding at the mouth where the bit has cut her. As the herd bears down on her, she whinnies her death song, a keening that cuts me like a woman's shriek, like the first screeches of an animal in a trap. Shrill and terrifyingly human. It's the last sound she makes as tree and horse drown in a black torrent.

There is nothing to do but study and wait them out. Unlike other beasts which depend on their legs to outrun danger, buffalo run with their tongues out, hungry for wind. They count on staying power as well as speed to outdistance what threatens them. So strong is this power that they can easily outrun a horse after a few miles. On the run, they close in a tight knot, the shoulders and haunches of one flush against those of its neighbors. Crushed together as they are, they aren't clumsy as you might expect but lumber forward with a terrible precision. Their pace doesn't slacken. Their gait is monotonous, unfaltering, so tight you could walk a bridge across their backs. And they make a chuffing noise as they run, something between panting and coughing. Though they must be spooked (God knows by what), they don't run helter-skelter but move in definite patterns. Each has and knows its place. Bulls, for instance, guard the flanks. Cows stick to the middle. The old bulls lag, bring up the rear. The calves, most of them larking, are everywhere, spanking their rope-like tails against their rumps as if to stir up more speed.

Twenty minutes it takes them to pass. The sound of falling rock dwindles to a droning echo, then is swallowed finally by distance. The whole landscape has changed. Where the sapling was, there are only splinters and shredded limbs. The ground where they passed is mangled, thrown up like a just-plowed field, but hashed, not creased with even furrows. And the mare. What's left of her is a deflated wreck, a pulp of raw meat and slackness, ruined. Where the spring lay in its pool is a mish-mash of mud and yellow water standing in ugly craters. Every leaf on my cottonwood is furred with dust.

Jacob Lewis

Come west to buy his sister
from captivity at Ft. Detroit,
Jacob Lewis of New Jersey
has an encounter with Girty
he won't soon forget.

When he enquires at Dr. Freeman's
the doctor cuts him short with
"Here comes Simon Girty."

Girty enters without knocking.
Face lush with malice,
turnip-red,
he saunters cross the room
and ripens,

eyes fast on the stranger's
until the latter asks
has he seen him before.

"No," the renegade replies,
"but if I ever see you again
I shall know you."

Then draws from its sheath
a long butcher knife

and throws it thunking
to the floor,
the bone handle humming,
its song in Lewis's ears
for what seems hours, days.

This act as punctuation.

Orville Hobbs, 1796

I CAN TELL YOU IT HAPPENED CAUSE I SAW IT. Wasn't I down the bankside there watching it all? Military everywhere. Blue coats milling through the streets. The ferry working double, taking loyalists over to British land. Old Glory over Detroit for the first time. Watching when this old gray-hair man comes riding up, beating his way through the crowd to the wharf, looking over his shoulder, hurried and high worried, I mean scared. Well, happens the ferryboat is halfway to Canada and he can't wait. So what does he do? He spurs that sucker off that high bank in a jump that puts them both in deep water, the head of the horse bobbing up first, then the man's. The two of them swimming for the Canada side of the river. Never saw a jump so proud. On the other shore, still mounted, sopping but safe, he jeers and swears a round of purple oaths, shakes his fist at the Americans and yells, Damn his bones but he won't give another inch. Not an inch.

Catherine Girty

SO LONG AS HE WAS SOBER he was good to me, though he was gone hunting or fighting much of the time. Traipsing over the country. He was not the picture of a family man, but he doted on the children, especially Prideaux, who was my last. Named for one of his bosom-companions.

After we married in Detroit, in August of '84 I think it was, we settled, if you can rightly say he ever settled. The place was Canada near Fort Malden. For his services to the Crown he claimed and was granted the farm, about 160 acres, which was at the head of Lake Erie a mile and a half below the fort. It was good land, mostly wooded. He is buried there. We lived in a log house with two windows and a door in front and one window in the end upstairs. All four children were born in this house.

It wasn't until after Prideaux was born in '97 that we separated. The reason was none other than his drinking. Sober, as I said, he was decent and even loving, a good provider. Drunk, he was a caution. Give him a nip he turned ugly and cruel, fuming and stamping around the house like a madman. When he struck me on the head with the flat of his sword—here, you can still see the scar—I left him, went to stay with my daughter at my son-in-law's. He kept a kind of tavern at Malden with rooms where I was always welcome.

Simon went from bad to worse. It was about this time that he broke his ankle while trying to jump a gate during one of his binges. The break never mended and he was lame in one leg for the rest of his days. At this time his sight was also going bad. Got so he wouldn't know you 10 feet away. He would mope around for days and stumble over chairs and things. Sometimes from drink, sometimes from his eyes. He was always what you might call moist. He wasn't able to work the farm any longer, not that he ever worked it much when he was able. But he was still drawing half-pay from the Crown and also did some interpreting from time to time.

Usually he could be found at the fort where liquor flowed freely. There he could always meet some of his Indian cronies. The bottle, I've always said, brought out the Indian in him. He would tear around on that old mare of his waving a war club, singing Indian songs, and filling the air with the sounds of the scalp halloo. Often, as long as he could, he would ride off on long hunts with them, the Indians I mean. Toward the end, even when he was crippled with rheumatism, he still rode off to hunt, bragging that he would breathe his last on a field of battle. Which, in a way, I guess he did.

1812

IN 1812, WHEN CHICKEN-LIVERED General William Hull surrendered Detroit to the British without a fight, Girty recrossed the river, this time by ferry. Sixteen years had passed since his hasty departure. Sixteen years older, he was seventy-two but hadn't really changed much as he boasted of his plunge into the river. Still defiant, still feisty, and as one observer put it, "drunk as usual."

Here's old blind Girty again on American soil, he shouted.

What came of the black mare carried you cross the water when Wayne was after you, a citizen asked.

O, she's dead, said Girty, and I buried her with all the honors of war.

Reconciliation

The sleep I sleep
is gorged with war,
my dreams are charred
as droves of bony widows
scrape their razors on my door,
lay orphans at my feet.

Waking now to milky light,
the cabin blanched with mutton snow,
my world made chaste again,
through window-glaze my breath melts
I squint to see my speckled hen,
that beauty
balanced on one sacrificial leg,
the other lifted snug in feathers
as she hops off one and then the other
in deference to the cold.

The truce she makes
I make my own.
I shift my stance
I change my gait,
I dress to suit the weather.

The perfect friction with the world
is snow that falls on water.

The Porch

SHAPES GRADUALLY GETTING DIMMER, each day a little dimmer. The dwarf elm 6 feet off my porch grows fuzz at first, goes wobbly in the limbs, then just melts.

What I sense now is not what I've always heard the blind do. Not some moonless dark without a dawn or center, bristles of light buried like preserves in some deep cellar in my head. No, my world is blanketed white, that gyrating gelid white you see when some blunt object strikes your closed eye. As the blow of a fist. Not just soupy white, but textured with a kind of grit which gives it depth. Rough like the surface of sandstone, but inviting to the touch. Not gloomy, as they say. The gloom is not being certain what comes next, or imagining what will. A fear of edges, sink-holes, low limbs, sleeping snakes. And after a week or so, after 75 years, this just doesn't worry me. I grow to trust the whiteness like a pillow. Black is not the color of my blooming.

Daniel Workman

IN 1816 I WENT TO MALDEN and put up at a hotel kept by a Frenchman [Peter Govereau]. I noticed in the barroom a gray-headed and blind old man. The landlady, who was his daughter [Ann], a woman of about thirty years of age, inquired of me, "Do you know who that is?" pointing to the old man. On my replying, "No," she rejoined, "It is Simon Girty." He had then been blind about four years.

Transitions

Strange and placid ways
in which the violent pass.
Some stroll through musket-storms
to die of bee-stings, allergies,
bad water.

Tom Girty, packing wounded British
from the field, just collapses.

Some die domestic.
McKee, 20 years a warhorse,
stepping out of bed
into his britches,
is butted by his pet deer,
the sharp tines
digging spigots in his rump—
and bleeds to death in minutes.

These deaths float gentle swarms
sift down in drowsy blizzards
on my sickbed.
I feel their snow,
each crystal build its winter
in my head,
the stiff blank petals
as they flake & pile,
flake & pile.

Basics

N'gattópui,

I am hungry.

N'gattosomi,

I am thirsty.

N'wiquihília,

I am tired, fatigued.

N'tschitannéssi,

I am strong.

N'schauwíhill,

I am weak, faint.

N'wischási,

I am afraid.

N'daptéssi,

I sweat.

N'dágotschi,

I am cold, freezing.

N'dellennówi,

I am a man.

N'dochquéwi,

I am a woman.

N'damándommen,

I feel.

N'leheléche,

I live, exist, draw breath.

CREDITS & SOURCES

MUCH OF *GIRTY* WAS WRITTEN with funds generously provided by a writing fellowship from the National Endowment for the Arts. The poem "November 1, 1779: First Snow" appeared in a slightly altered version in *The Small Farm*. "The Meadow" was reprinted in *Woods and Waters: A Kentucky Outdoors Reader*, edited by Ron Ellis, University Press of Kentucky, 2005. The first edition of *Girty* was published by Turtle Island Foundation of Berkeley, California in 1977, the second by Gnomon Press in 1990. The late Charlie Hughes of Wind Publications printed a third edition of *Girty* in 2006 to which Ted Franklin Belue's introduction was added.

An earlier version in two parts was printed in *Adena, A Journal of the History and Culture of the Ohio River Valley*.

The richest single source of material on Simon Girty is Consul Willshire Butterfield's *History of the Girtys* (Cincinnati, 1890). Daniel Workman's words are transcribed from it. So is the excerpt from Frank Cowan's poem. Several parts of *Girty* are drawn from primary sources. The description of Bryan's Station is from Henry Howe's *Historical Recollections of the Great West* (Cincinnati, 1873). The "Account of the Capture and Torture of Col. William Crawford" appeared in *Knight's and Slover's Narratives* (1783). The interview with Simon Kenton is from F. W. Thomas's *Sketches and Tales* (Louisville, 1849). The conjugation of the Delaware verb "to burn" was taken from Henry R. Schoolcraft's *Indian Tribes of the United States* (Philadelphia, 1852). The Delaware words on the last page were selected from the list compiled by Rev. John Heckewelder in *History, Manners, and Customs of the Indian Nations* (Philadelphia, 1819). The speeches brought by Girty to Detroit and the inventory of plunder from Rogers' keelboats were adapted from *Frontier Advance on the Upper Ohio: 1778–1779*, Volume IV, Draper Series, ed. Louise Kellogg (Madison, Wisconsin, 1916). The rhetoric of Girty's egg speech is taken from Allan W. Eckert's *The Frontiersmen* (Boston, 1967). The passage fictionalizing Girty's disaffection from his wife is reprinted from Uriah Jones' *Simon Girty, the Outlaw: An Historical Romance* (Philadelphia, 1846). The estimate of Girty's life is from Edwin P. Thompson's *Young People's History of Kentucky* (St. Louis, 1897). The cane and clover speech was spoken by Girty to the assembled tribes at the Grand Council at Chillecothe, Ohio, before marching on Bryan's Station in 1782. It is reprinted from Julian Campbell's unpublished dissertation, *The Land of Cane and Clover, Presettlement Vegetation in the So-Called Bluegrass Region of Kentucky*, University of Kentucky, 1985.

Other useful sources were John Bakeless's *Daniel Boone* (New York, 1939); Richard Banta's *The Ohio* (New York, 1949); Wallace Brice's *History of Fort Wayne* (Fort Wayne, Indiana, 1868); Thomas Boyd's *Simon Girty: The White Savage* (New York, 1928); Mann Butler's *Valley of the Ohio* (1855) (reprinted Frankfort, Kentucky, 1971); Consul Willshire Butterfield's *An Historical Account of the Expedition against Sandusky under Col. William Crawford in 1782* (Cincinnati, 1873); George Morgan Chinn's *Kentucky's Settlement and Statehood: 1750–1800* (Frankfort, 1975); Lewis Collins' *Kentucky* (Cincinnti, 1847), David Dary's *The Buffalo Book* (New York, 1974); John McClung's *Sketches of Western Adventures* (Maysville, Kentucky, 1832); *Pioneer History* (Historical Society of Cincinnati,

1848); Emilius 0. Randall's *History of Ohio*, Volumes I, II (New York, 1912); George W. Ranck's *Girty, the White Indian* (New York, 1886); Thomas Speed's *The Wilderness Road* (New York, 1886, 1971); Walter W. Spooner's *The Backwoodsmen* (Cincinnati, 1883); and John R. Swanton's *The Indian Tribes of North America* (Washington, D.C., 1952).

ABOUT THE AUTHOR

RICHARD TAYLOR is Keenan Visiting Writer at Transylvania University where he has taught creative writing and English since 2008. He has published a number of collections of poetry with historic themes, drawing on the lives of Abraham Lincoln, John James Audubon, and Cassius M. Clay, hand-printed by Larkpur Press in Monterey, Kentucky. In addition to *Girty*, he has written a second novel, *Sue Mundy: A Novel of the Civil War* (University Press of Kentucky, 2006), and several books relating to Kentucky history, including *The Great Crossing: A Historic Journey to Buffalo Trace Distillery*, *The Palisades of the Kentucky River*, and *Elkhorn: Evolution of a Kentucky Landscape*. winner of the 2018 Thomas D. Clark Medallion and a Kentucky Historical Society Publication Award. From 1999-2001 Taylor served as Kentucky's poet laureate. He is currently working on a collection of personal essays whose working title is "Fathers." He lives on a small farm near Frankfort and is co-owner of Poor Richard's Books.